Catherine Collor

GW00730004

G

Everything is going marvellously for Gemma until her mother's announcement. She's coming home and Gemma will have to go back to London. But how can Gemma leave Headstone now? She's going to play Juliet with the most exciting Romeo—she *can't* just walk out on the play.

And what about her cousins? Ann is practically a pop star and Lydia's more determined than ever to be a prima ballerina. Then there's Robin whose career needs a boost. Poor Gemma, she hadn't expected to become so attached to her 'ordinary' family . . .

Also by Noel Streatfeild in Fontana Lions

Gemma
Gemma and Sisters
Gemma Alone
When the Siren Wailed
Ballet Shoes for Anna
Thursday's Child
Far to Go
A Vicarage Family

First published in 1969
First published in Fontana Lions 1973
8 Grafton Street, London W1X 3LA
Ninth impression April 1986

Fontana Lions is an imprint of
Fontana Paperbacks, part of
the Collins Publishing Group

Copyright © Noel Streatfeild 1969

Printed in Great Britain
by William Collins Sons & Co. Ltd, Glasgow

Conditions of Sale
This book is sold subject to the condition
that it shall not, by way of trade or otherwise,
be lent, re-sold, hired out or otherwise circulated
without the publisher's prior consent in any form of
binding or cover other than that in which it is
published and without a similar condition
including this condition being imposed
on the subsequent purchaser

Goodbye
Gemma

Noel Streatfeild

Illustrated by Betty Maxey

FONTANA LIONS

CONTENTS

CHAPTER ONE

NEWS FOR GEMMA

THE Dean of Headstone University looked with approval at the façade of The School of Drama and Stage Training. It was two Victorian houses knocked into one and he liked Victoriana, which he found a pleasant change from the very up-to-date functional buildings which Headstone had caused to be erected for its first university. He wished as he rang the bell that he would find Mrs. Calvert, the headmistress, a piece of Victoriana too, but that was too much to hope. Stage ladies—as he described them to himself—had never come his way, for which he was grateful for he was sure they were alarming.

Mrs. Calvert, when the Dean was shown into her sitting-room, was a pleasant surprise. She had perhaps not a Victorian but certainly an Edwardian look, due possibly, he thought, to the almost period style in which she wore her red hair.

"Good afternoon, Dean," she said. "Do sit down. Tea is just coming."

The Dean sat.

"It is very kind of you to spare time for a stranger."

Mrs. Calvert smiled.

"You don't feel like a stranger. We heard so much about you when you were appointed and of course I was at the opening ceremony, it was a great day here—the very first time royalty has visited Headstone."

The Dean nodded.

"Strange, for Headstone is only one hundred and fifty miles from London and has so much of which to be proud: St. Giles, both the church and the choir school

5

and, of course, The Steen orchestra is world famous, and I hear the music school is excellent."

Tea arrived and Mrs. Calvert poured the Dean out a cup and passed him a plate of scones.

"Home-made and, I think you will agree, excellent. Now, tell me what I can do for you? You are a busy man so it must be important for you to find time to visit me."

The Dean put down his cup.

"Did you hear we produced a very creditable performance of 'Hamlet' last year?"

"Naturally. I hear it was quite an achievement and that you have a really outstanding actor in the young man who played Hamlet."

"That is the point. John Cann is outstanding—so outstanding I felt he should be encouraged. Mrs. Calvert, he wants to play Romeo."

Mrs. Calvert was puzzled. Why shouldn't the university struggle with "Romeo and Juliet" if they had managed "Hamlet"?

"A worthy ambition," she said.

"Indeed yes," agreed the Dean, "but, as things are, impossible. You see Headstone University cannot produce a Juliet."

"Are you sure? Surely amongst all those young women one must be teachable."

"We shall want a young woman who is more than just teachable if she is to perform opposite John Cann."

"What about whoever played Ophelia in your last production?" Mrs. Calvert asked.

"She has left and she would not have been up to it. The drama group has auditioned every girl who is willing from our new entrants and the result has been most disappointing—most." The Dean gave a thin smile. "We seem to attract brawn rather than dramatic ability. That

6

was why it was suggested I come to you. Have you a Juliet you could lend us?"

Mrs. Calvert refilled the Dean's cup.

"Have you heard of Gemma Bow?"

The Dean shook his head.

"Should I have?"

Mrs. Calvert passed him another scone.

"Not unless you go to the cinema or watch television."

The Dean looked apologetic.

"I never go to the cinema and as a rule I only watch television when there is cricket."

Mrs. Calvert had expected that answer.

"Gemma Bow is the daughter of Rowena Alston. She was a film star and is now starring in a T/V series in the United States. Gemma was a very successful child actress in films. But when her mother left for California she was not working so she was sent to live with relatives in Headstone. You may have come across them. Their name is Robinson . . ."

"Philip Robinson?" the Dean asked. "He was I know with The Steen. He teaches some of our musical scholars."

"That's the one. Mrs. Robinson is Rowena Alston's sister so she took Gemma into the family and sent her with her eldest girl to Headstone Comprehensive. There, under the name of Gemma Robinson, she made quite a name for herself as an amateur actress, first in a school pageant and then as Lady Jane Grey."

"I have heard of the production of Lady Jane Grey, it is still talked about. Written by a local school teacher I understand."

"That is correct. Gemma Robinson, as she was then called, gave a good performance by any standards but startling in an amateur, for no one knew she was really Gemma Bow."

7

"Then she was sent to you?"

"Yes, but not only as an actress. It was her uncle, Philip Robinson, who wanted her to come to me. He felt Gemma was not the type of child to do well in a Comprehensive, she needed a far smaller school with much individual attention. Last term she played Rosalind in our end of term production. She had done very little Shakespeare but at the performance I saw real promise."

The Dean was delighted.

"Now you feel she could play Juliet?"

"Yes, she is already studying the part and she is just Juliet's age, but whether she can act in your production time will tell. She is playing the lead in a T/V series which is showing on Sundays. It is a film version of 'Rebecca of Sunnybrook Farm'. She is excellent as Rebecca so it will not surprise me if there are further offers."

"Oh dear," said the Dean, "and she cannot be persuaded to refuse them? I can promise her to act with John Cann will be an experience, he is I am sure a future Laurence Olivier."

Mrs. Calvert finished her cup of tea before she answered.

"A chance to play Juliet could be helpful for it will not be Gemma who wishes to accept further engagements but her mother. So the more ammunition Gemma has with which to persuade her mother the better her chances are of remaining in my care." Mrs. Calvert pushed a bell. "You shall see Gemma. But don't think, if she plays Juliet opposite your young man, the good fortune will be all on her side for he too will be in luck. I believe Gemma could be a future Peggy Ashcroft."

Gemma was having a French lesson when she was told she was wanted in Mrs. Calvert's room. Asking to be excused she gave her head a shake to make her fair hair fall becomingly over her shoulders, gave a tug to the black

8

linen pinafore dress which was the drama school's uniform for the girls and went into the passage.

The girl who had brought the message was waiting outside. Though she was senior to Gemma she was pleased to have a talk with her for Gemma was considered special by the whole school. It was not only that she had been a film star when she was younger, or even that she could now be seen each Sunday starring in "Rebecca of Sunnybrook Farm", it was because there was something about her which made her stand out. A sort of aura of success.

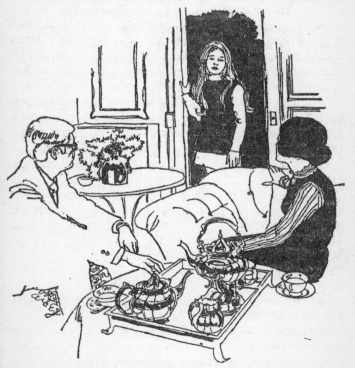

"Gemma, this is the Dean of the University."

"Have you been going out with one of the university boys?" the girl asked.

Gemma had not yet reached the stage of being dated so she laughed at the question.

"No. Why?"

"Because the Dean of the university is with Mrs. Calvert."

Gemma was far too used to meeting people to be impressed, nor did she even wonder why the Dean wanted to see her. Probably, she supposed, he had a child who was watching Rebecca who wanted an autograph.

The Dean was surprised when he first saw Gemma. She stood in the doorway—a child in a black pinafore—a very pretty child but a child looking, as so many children did, bored at being taken from what she was doing, to talk to grown-ups.

"Gemma," said Mrs. Calvert, "this is the Dean of the university. He is looking for a Juliet to play opposite a very talented Romeo."

Gemma came forward to shake the Dean's hand and, as she did so, the Dean saw the most startling change come over her. It was as if a brilliant light were switched on inside her and was shining out of her.

"I read the play last term," she told him, "and this term Mrs. Calvert is working at it with me three days a week, but of course I'm working at Juliet on my own as well."

"You are very young," said the Dean.

"So was Juliet," Gemma retorted. "As a matter of fact I'm the same age as she was."

"If Gemma plays Juliet," Mrs. Calvert asked, "when would rehearsals start?"

The Dean was still looking at Gemma, trying to imagine her dressed as Juliet.

"Not regularly until after Christmas. The performance will not be until May."

Mrs. Calvert looked approving.

"Good—that will give us time to have worked at the whole play. I don't believe in taking scenes out of context. I suggest we wait until Gemma has studied the balcony scene before you produce your young man."

The Dean could see Mrs. Calvert was not one to argue with. He had found what he had come for—perhaps a little young but there was certainly something about the child. He got up.

"That is settled then. I will inform the drama group they can go ahead with 'Romeo and Juliet' and you will inform me when you wish Gemma to meet John Cann."

CHAPTER TWO

NEWS FOR THE BOYS

THE Robinsons lived in a Victorian house which was part of a row called Trelawny Drive. To other people it might seem to be just one house in a rather ugly row but the Robinsons—and they included Gemma—never thought how the house looked for to them it was just home.

The evening of the day Gemma had heard about acting Juliet the children were converging on Trelawny Drive on their way home from their different schools. First came Ann on her bicycle from the comprehensive, a bulging satchel of homework on her back. It had been Ann's father's hope that she would try for a scholarship at The Royal College of Music for she had a beautiful singing voice, but that was not what Ann wanted. She had no ambition to be in the public eye, her dream was to go to Oxford. Now, however, her mind was fixed on tea. Her mother worked half days at Headstone Hospital.

which meant she did not get home until about six, so Ann got the family tea. "I do hope," she thought as she pushed her bicycle into the shed that her father had built as a garage when on his retirement from The Steen he had been presented with a car, "we get tea over quickly. I do want plenty of time for my homework."

Gemma and her younger cousin Lydia—always known as Lydie—went to the same school. Lydia was not an ordinary drama school pupil for she was there as part of a scholarship awarded her by her dancing teacher, Miss Arrowhead. Lydia seemed to soak up news as blotting paper soaks up ink so she greeted Gemma with:

"Why did you see the Dean of the university?"

Gemma laughed.

"You won't think it very interesting. It was about me playing Juliet in the university's production of 'Romeo and Juliet'."

"Why you?" Lydia asked. "Heaps of girls go there."

"I don't know but Mrs. Calvert said they have a very talented Romeo."

Lydia thought this over.

"I don't know why everything happens to you. Here's me day after day doing the same old exercises with Miss Arrowhead, no one ever wants me to dance in a ballet. But you have only got to learn a part and you are acting it properly. Rosalind last term and now Juliet this."

"It's not this term it's next May."

"Still, you know you're going to act it. Now me, Miss Arrowhead sometimes says things like 'You'll need perfect balance if you are to dance Aurora. Think of the rose adagio', but not as something that is going to happen but only which might happen."

Robin, the youngest of the Robinsons, was delayed coming home. Just as he and his red-headed friend Nigs Gamesome were leaving the choir school they were given a message to say the choirmaster wished to see them.

"Bother!" said Robin quickly thinking over any sins he might have committed. "What does he want?"

The choirmaster was waiting for them in the chapel. He did not, the boys were thankful to notice, look cross.

"Ah boys!" he said. "I've a letter here about you." He took a letter from his pocket. "Who is Barry Thomas?"

Robin gave Nigs a look to say "leave this to me". Mr. Reynolds, the choirmaster, was a good musician and quite nice when you got to know him, but he had, the boys thought, a one-track mind—no modern music except Benjamin Britten was worth singing.

"Well, sir," Robin explained, "my sister and Nigs and me and my cousin Gemma have an act we call Gemma and Sisters, which we do for charity. We've done it for ages."

Mr. Reynolds knew about Gemma and Sisters.

"You sing folk tunes I understand which you have had the audacity to mess about to produce that sound you call swirled."

"There's other things, sir," Nigs broke in. "Ann, Robin's eldest sister, sings really well and she does a solo absolutely straight—well Mr. Robinson accompanies her and you know how fussy he is."

Mr. Reynolds was an admirer of Philip's.

"I don't but I think fussy an ill-chosen word."

Robin took up the story again.

"Then my younger sister does a dance and my cousin Gemma sings to a banjo. I accompany my own swirled songs, which the girls sing, and Nigs helps out with a bit of drumming."

"None of which explains who Barry Thomas is," said Mr. Reynolds.

Robin took a deep breath.

"Dad is going to write to you about it. You remember,

13

sir, last term you gave permission for me and Nigs to go in for that talent contest on T/V which we didn't win? Well, after it, this Mr. Barry Thomas rang up and said he could get us the chance to make a record. He wrote to Nigs' father and we're going to make it soon."

"Ah!" said Mr. Reynolds. "Now I see the picture. It seems there is now discussion about the reverse side of your record. Mr. Thomas writes they are wondering if there might be some suitable church music for you as solo boy with the choir."

Nigs gave Robin a slap on the back.

"I told you that you should make a record of 'O for the wings of a dove'."

"That," said Mr. Reynolds, "would seem to be what Mr. Barry Thomas has in mind. He also suggests the song 'Matthew, Mark, Luke and John'. I must get in touch with your fathers. It would seem that most of the arrangements have been made with your father, Nigel?"

"That's right, sir," Nigs agreed. "You see, the man who got us tried out for the T/V contest was a Rotarian like Dad."

Mr. Reynolds went on as if Nigs had not spoken.

"There is a great deal to be discussed, of course, but it might be possible to agree to Mr. Barry Thomas' request."

There was always a lot of talk in the evening. So much seemed to happen between breakfast and Philip and Alice coming home. That day they were hardly inside the front door before Robin and Nigs were pouring out their news. As both Nigs and Robin talked at the same time at first it was hard to sort out what had happened, except the news seemed to be good. At last, after several one at a time pleas, Philip got the story.

"That sounds as though they were getting down to that record at last. I'm glad as it will make up for your disappointment at not coming top in the talent contest. You tell your father all this when you get home, Nigs, perhaps he'd go round to the choir school and have a talk with Mr. Reynolds."

Gemma came running down the stairs.

"Oh, Uncle Philip! The Dean of the university came to see Mrs. Calvert today. They are putting on 'Romeo and Juliet' next term and I am to be Juliet."

Philip kissed her.

"Well, that is wonderful news. But why you? The university is full of young women."

"I know," Gemma agreed. "I was surprised but the Dean didn't say why. Mrs. Calvert said he wanted someone to play opposite a very talented Romeo. His name is John Cann."

Philip had not taught the violin to university students for nothing.

"I know about him. I gather he's something quite out of the ordinary. When they put on 'Hamlet' *The Times* sent their critic down to see the performance, he gave John Cann a wonderful write-up."

Alice, who had taken off her coat and was on her way to get the supper, smiled lovingly at Gemma.

"This is exciting news. It will be the first time you've had a clever young man to act with, won't it?"

Gemma thought about that.

"I suppose it will. There were lots of clever men in my pictures but it wasn't like having a good Romeo."

Lydia, who had been practising her dancing, was coming down the stairs so she heard what Gemma said.

"You had that marvellous Orlando last term."

Everybody laughed. The boy who had played Orlando last term had proved a very dull actor.

"Have you heard the boys' news, Lydie," her father asked.

15

"Of course, all through tea."

"I think it may concern you girls," Philip said. "For if they are thinking of having Robin and the choir on the reverse side it sounds as though they were making a long-playing record and not a single as we had supposed."

Gemma gasped.

"Goodness, that will mean all the songs we sing in Gemma and Sisters."

"Well, you must certainly have them ready," Philip agreed, "We had better have a rehearsal on Saturday. Can you make that, Nigs?"

"That's O.K.," Nigs agreed. "But it won't make much difference, will it? I mean we should soon have had to start rehearsals for Gemma and Sisters for the Christmas holidays, shouldn't we?"

Alice turned to Gemma.

"Come and help me get the supper and tell me more about the Dean."

Lydia was going to offer to come too when she remembered something.

"My goodness! I hadn't remembered it would soon be Christmas. I must ask Miss Arrowhead to teach me the dance on my pointes. Really it's only sort of reminding her because when I asked her last term she almost promised that she would. Oh Dad, imagine on my pointes! I can hardly wait for Christmas for the Gemma and Sisters concerts to start."

CHAPTER THREE

DOUBTS AND FEARS

IN a family one member being in a mood upsets the contentment of all. For the rest of that week Lydia had a mood and upset everybody, but it was not until the rehearsal on Saturday that her mood came to a head.

Philip, as usual when it was a music rehearsal, was in charge.

"I shall have to time each song separately," he explained, "but as a start let's run through the lot. Which will you begin with, Robin?"

There were four songs that Robin had swirled. "O dear, what can the matter be?" The song about the little woman who had her skirts cut up to her knees. "Aiken Drum" and "The Four Presents" with its refrain "Perrie, merrie, dixie and domine".

"Could we start with 'The Four Presents'?" Robin asked. "It gives Nigs a great warm up on the drums, then 'O dear, what can the matter be?'—then the little woman and finish with 'Aiken Drum'."

"Right," Philip agreed. He looked at Gemma and Lydia. "Have you got that?"

There was no need to ask Ann. She sang in the church choir and her school choir and was an experienced soloist, so she never missed a musical direction.

Gemma never missed a stage direction and a singing rehearsal taken by Uncle Philip was to her the same thing so she answered briskly:

"O.K. I've got it."

Lydia had turned pink and seemed about to explode.

"I've got it but I don't agree and I don't see why Robin should decide, it's us that is going to sing."

Philip was puzzled but knowing Lydia was in a mood he handled her carefully.

"What don't you agree with, Lydie?"

Lydia didn't really know except that she wanted to disagree with everything.

"Well, why start with 'The Four Presents'? It's much the most difficult."

17

"I told you," Robin said, "because of Nigs on the drums."

Ann tried to help.

"It was difficult once but not now you know it."

Gemma joined in.

"It's true, Lydie. The perrie, merrie, dixies were awful at first but you and I never get them wrong now."

Philip looked at Lydia.

"I think that disposes of that, Lydie. Now shall we start?"

"It doesn't dispose of anything," Lydia shouted. "Nothing at all." Then she burst into tears.

Robin and Nigs gave each other a long-suffering look which said "Girls!". The others gathered round Lydia trying to find out what was wrong.

"What is it, darling?" Alice asked. "Aren't you feeling well?"

Philip put an arm round her.

"What's the trouble, old lady? Something has been worrying you all the week, hasn't it?"

"It's nothing to do with the songs, is it Lydie?" Ann whispered. "Come on, tell us what's wrong."

Gemma, her mind on Juliet, had not noticed Lydia's mood as much as the others. But now she saw her crying she guessed where the trouble lay. There was only one thing Lydia was likely to cry about.

"Aren't you being allowed to dance on your pointes?"

A sort of howl came out of Lydia.

"I don't know what's wrong for Miss Arrowhead as good as promised last term. So on Wednesday I said please could she start to teach me the dance for Gemma and Sisters and she said . . . "

Whatever Miss Arrowhead had said was lost in a gale of sobs.

"Come on, darling, stop crying and tell us what she said."

It took time but at last Lydia got it out.

"She was queer, she didn't exactly look at me and then she said—she said . . ."

"Go on, Lydie, tell us," Philip urged.

Lydie swallowed a sob.

"She said she was terribly sorry but she was afraid there could be nothing new this side of Christmas. She said: 'You've got a repertoire of character dances. They'll have to do'."

Her family, even Robin, were dismayed. There had been so much trouble over Lydia's dances in the show, mostly caused by Lydia herself. She had danced in the first shows without permission from Miss Arrowhead, which was against the rules. Then, when she was caught, she had agreed never to dance unless the dance had been rehearsed by Miss Arrowhead. Lydia had faithfully stuck to this for a time then, for a special concert, without permission, she had danced on her pointes and Miss Arrowhead had been in the audience. There had been a terrible punishment for that, for one whole term Miss Arrowhead had refused to teach her but had left her to her niece, Polly, who taught beginners and the less talented. That punishment had a great effect on Lydia, who had worked in a most disciplined way very hard since. As a result she had Miss Arrowhead's half promise of the dance on her pointes at Christmas. Whatever could have happened for Miss Arrowhead to have changed her mind for she must have known how much Lydia was counting on that half promise?

"Oh, poor Lydie! What a shame!" said Ann.

Philip was turning over what Lydia had told them. It sounded to him as if Miss Arrowhead was in trouble of some sort, trouble that might be taking up her spare time.

"It's quite a long way to Christmas. If Miss Arrowhead is too busy just now to think of new dances perhaps she can be persuaded to teach you one a little later on."

Lydia saw a ray of hope.

"Will you ask her, Dad? She listens to you."

"Not just now if she's got a lot on but in a week or two I'll have a word with her."

Lydia was the mercurial type. With her father's promise to see Miss Arrowhead her misery evaporated. Almost she could see herself not only dancing on her pointes but wearing a tutu which, wrapped in cellophane, had been hanging in a cupboard unworn since the Christmas before last when Gemma's mother had sent it to her from America. Really Lydia knew perfectly well she could not wear her tutu in Gemma and Sisters for the three girls were dressed alike, but she was sure, once she had learned to dance on her pointes, she would find an occasion to dance wearing it. So, even before her tears had dried, she was beaming at her father.

"All right. I'm ready to sing now and really I don't care a bit which order we sing the songs in."

Partly because of the expense but largely because he felt the children had better things to do than watch television Philip had never had a television set. But when Gemma's mother heard from Gemma that the family were appearing in a talent contest she sent them the set she was going to give them later in the year on which to watch "Rebecca of Sunnybrook Farm". Viewing was not permitted during the working week because of homework, but the children were allowed to view at the weekends, and sometimes after they were in bed Philip and Alice would look at the box and were surprised how much entertainment they got from it.

20

"I had always supposed I would enjoy concerts," Philip confessed to Alice, "but I'm bound to say I find a lot of it most amusing and very relaxing."

Sundays found all the family gathered round the set at least five minutes before "Rebecca of Sunnybrook Farm" started, Ann and Robin ready to fly off to join their choirs the moment the serial finished. Gemma was always slightly nervous. The serial was proving popular, how awful if this Sunday wasn't up to standard! Then there was her own performance. No actress, however experienced, is ever satisfied with her appearance and performance on T/V, there are always places where she wishes she had worn a different expression or said a line differently, and Gemma was no exception. The maddening thing was that she had found she had to keep her criticisms to herself for none of the Robinsons had any idea what she was talking about.

The Sunday after the rehearsal even Gemma could not discover much to find fault with. It was the scene where she and her great friend Emma Jane drive round the countryside selling soap to win a lamp for a poor family. It was also the scene in which Rebecca met for the first time the man the film story was to suggest she would some day marry. Not that there was a hint about that in this scene, where Rebecca was still an eager little girl.

All the family—even Ann who had secretly thought the story rather a bore—enjoyed that sequence and they thought Gemma marvellously good. As soon as it was over and Ann and Robin had dashed off Philip said:

"I shouldn't allow that poor Dean to count on you too much for Juliet. I feel it in my bones this serial is going to open new doors for you."

"But you know that isn't what I want," Gemma retorted. "I want to stay where I am and work at Juliet."

"But what about Aunt Rowena?" said Lydia. "She's the one who will decide, isn't she?"

That put Gemma on her high horse.

"She won't interefere with me, it's my life."

Alice exchanged a glance with Philip.

"That's true, of course, but I wouldn't feel absolutely sure that you can stay at the drama school, darling. I expect your mother is ambitious for you and you can't blame her, can you?"

Gemma refused to listen.

"I'm going to act Juliet and nobody is going to stop me."

Lydia, stiff from sitting down, turned a couple of pirouettes.

"Fatal last words," she said.

CHAPTER FOUR

ANN

BARRY THOMAS was to bring a man called Eli Push to Headstone for the week-end. He was part owner of the recording company which was to make the record. Barry Thomas and Eli Push were coming primarily to hear the choir with Robin as solo boy sing, and to see George Gamesome about the contract for the record of the swirled songs, but making the arrangements on the telephone Barry Thomas had said:

"Eli Push probably won't want to hear Robin's swirled stuff again as he heard it on T/V, but he just might so tell the kids to stand by."

This in the T/V world was normal behaviour. Nobody connected with T/V could suppose that anyone they wanted to use was not constantly at their beck and call. It was not, however, usual behaviour in the Robinson family so when George Gamesome passed on the message there was argument from, of all people, Ann.

For two never to be forgotten holidays the family had stayed at a farm called Torworthy in Devonshire. There they had met another family called Stratford. The Stratfords had a daughter called Audrey who had become Ann's closest friend. Neither Ann nor Audrey made friends easily so the friendship was encouraged by both families and it had become the custom for Ann to stay with Audrey for half-term holidays. The week-end Barry Thomas was to bring Eli Push to Headstone was Ann's half-term. So the moment she heard Barry Thomas' message she said:

"I'm not giving up my half-term with Audrey. I mean it's all planned."

Alice was entirely with her.

"Of course you can't. I don't suppose Mr. Push will want to hear the songs again but if he does we must manage without you. You two could get along on your own, couldn't you?"

Philip had to interrupt.

"I expect you're right about Mr. Push not wanting to hear them again but Gemma and Lydia couldn't manage without Ann."

"Well, get someone else to sing," Alice said. "I don't see why Ann should have her holiday upset."

Robin tried to make his mother understand.

"My swirled songs are written in two parts, Mum. Ann sings one part and Gemma and Lydie the other."

Philip spoke firmly.

"It's out of the question the songs being sung without Ann and I'm afraid the programme is too short so there will be new songs to learn."

"Well tell Mr. Thomas that week-end isn't convenient." Alice suggested. "I expect he can choose another."

Gemma nearly laughed.

"Heads of gramophone companies and T/V people aren't used to being told things like that."

"If only we had room," said Ann, "we could squeeze Audrey in here. I expect the Stratfords wouldn't mind and she's never been to Headstone, but Dad's doing up the spare room."

It was then that Gemma had a good idea. She turned to Robin.

"The Gamesomes would have you to stay, wouldn't they? Then I could move into your room and Audrey can share with Ann."

Alice almost clapped her hands.

"What a wonderful idea! You'd like to have her here, Ann, wouldn't you?"

Ann always had a marvellous time staying with the Stratfords but it was right that Audrey should stay with her, so she was quite happy at the change of plans and really she had known Gemma and Lydia couldn't manage the songs without her.

Philip was thankful Ann had agreed for he had timed the songs and knew they would not be long enough to make, as now seemed likely, an L.P. He had been searching for something suitable to fill in though his choice had, of course, to be approved by Robin. That evening he brought Robin a song book.

"Do you think this would swirl?" he asked, opening the book at "The Frog's Wooing".

Robin could play most tunes at sight. He played the tune through, then he shook his head.

"The girls will never learn all those words in a hurry."

"I've thought of that," said Philip. "Why not have a change and let Ann sing all the words and Gemma and Lydie can join in on the Heigh-ho's?"

Robin played the song through again while Philip sang the words and he joined in with the Heigh-ho's.

"Not bad," he said, "not bad at all, at least it won't be when it's swirled."

Robin intended to start his swirling right away but Philip stopped him.

"I reckon we shall want two more songs at least so how about this?" "This" was an old nursery rhyme called "Ye Frog and Ye Crow". "I suggest—when you've swirled it—Ann sings this quite alone—without even the drums."

Robin played the music through and was pleased with it.

"It's full of possibilities, Dad—it would swirl well."

"Good!" said Philip. "Then I'll tell Ann to learn the songs. We'll separate them so they don't upset the balance of the programme."

To her father's surprise—knowing how Ann disliked singing in public—she made no objection to the two solos.

"There's too many words for us all to learn them by half-term," she agreed, "but I'll learn them and then find time to go through them with Robin when they're swirled."

"It's good of you, darling," said Philip, "for I know you don't like solos and on top of giving up going to the Stratfords it's a lot to ask."

"I don't mind this sort of solo," Ann explained. "There's no stage to get on and off and no bowing, and now I've got used to the idea I'm glad Audrey is coming here and she sounded thrilled on the telephone."

Barry Thomas arranged with Mr. Reynolds to hear the choir at their usual Friday evening practice.

"Eli Push says he would like to hear the children the next morning," Barry Thomas said on the telephone, "so he can get back to London in the afternoon."

At first everybody was inclined to argue. It meant Philip putting off a pupil. It meant Gemma missing a banjo lesson with Ted Smith. It meant Lydia missing her Saturday dancing class with Miss Arrowhead. But after a lot of "Not Saturday morning!" "You know I can't manage Saturday mornings!" the arguments died down and everybody agreed that singing on Saturday morning was not as earth-shaking as they had at first imagined.

"I suppose I can squeeze my pupil in for an extra lesson next week," Philip said.

Gemma telephoned Ted and arranged for extra time the following Saturday.

"As a matter of fact," Lydia said, "Miss Arrowhead didn't take the class last week, Polly did, and if she's taking it I don't care how often I miss it." She looked at her father. "Polly taking the Saturday class for Miss Arrowhead is another odd thing. I do hope you'll see Miss Arrowhead soon, Dad, about my dance for Gemma and Sisters."

There was a recording studio in Headstone. It was small and could not manage a large group but there was just enough room for the children, the grand piano and Nigs' drums. It was rather cosy in there on their own and they all felt nice and relaxed. Philip had helped Robin with the programme order. They began with "The Four Presents", then Ann's solo "The Frog's Wooing", then "O dear, what can the matter be?" followed by "The Little Woman", then Ann's second solo "Ye Frog and Ye Crow", and they finished in grand style with "Aiken Drum".

When they had finished the recording Robin waited for the light to turn from red to green, then he said triumphantly:

"I thought we were smashing."

They had all thought they were smashing so they came

out of the recording room expecting a shower of praise. Instead no one noticed they had come out. Both Mr. Push and Barry Thomas were in a corner talking to Philip, and to be sure he was listening one held one lapel of his coat and one the other. It looked as though Philip was trying to argue and getting nowhere. The only person who noticed the children was Nigs' father, who was not much help when it came to saying how they had sounded. However, he was better than no one.

"Were we all right?" Lydia asked him.

Mr. Gameson shook his head.

"Now why ask me? You know I don't know one note from another, but they liked it." He jabbed a finger at the group in the corner.

Robin turned to look at his father.

"Then what's the fuss about?"

George Gamesome lowered his voice.

"It's something to do with you, Ann. That odd-looking fellow Push practically hit the ceiling when you sang alone. He said something about the voice of the century."

"What a fool!" said Ann. "I wish they'd let Dad go. I want to get home. Audrey and I are going to the pictures."

CHAPTER FIVE

IT ISN'T FAIR

ROBIN was one of those types for whom life seems easy. Without much effort he had done well at the choir school. He had a good true voice so with remarkable speed had risen to be solo boy. He had quite adequate brains so without undue slogging he kept near the top of his form. He had an eye for a ball and so did well at games. On top of these gifts he had an easy friendly nature, which

27

meant he got on well with both masters and boys. Other parents would say enviously:

"Robin's such an easy child."

But when Philip heard this he would say to Alice:

"I do hope life isn't being too easy for Robin, for if he ever gets a knock he is going to find it hard to take."

Now Robin had to take a knock and, as his father had feared, he had nothing in his make-up to cope with it. The recording of his swirled songs had been the biggest thing that had ever happened to him. He and Nigs had dreamed of his record being top of the pops. Of swirled music becoming the latest craze.

"And imagine," Nigs had said, "if it is a craze you are absolutely the only person in the world who knows how to swirl. Why you might make Headstone as famous as The Beatles made Liverpool."

The higher their hopes rose the greater the fall when the news broke. Robin's record was now to be a single of "Ye Frog and Ye Crow". There was to be no Nigs on the drums and no Gemma or Lydia, it was, as Mr. Eli Push explained, a means of introducing Ann to what he was sure would be her worshipping public.

"But, Dad," said Robin, "it isn't fair. It was to be my very own record called 'The Robinson Family'. Barry Thomas said so. Now it's all Ann. It isn't fair."

Philip nodded.

"I couldn't agree with you more. It isn't fair. But I'm afraid life never is. Millionaires who don't want the money win sweepstakes and people like Ann, who never wanted to make a record, find themselves making one."

"If she didn't want to make one why didn't she say she wouldn't do it?"

Philip tried to explain.

"It wasn't easy. Mr. Push held, as it were, a pistol to her head. If she wouldn't sign on the dotted line—or rather if I wouldn't sign for her—there was to be no choir music and, as you know, St. Giles needs the money."

"They are going to make an L.P.," Robin growled, "but I bet nobody buys it."

"They will," said Philip. "Mr. Eli Push is not a fool. One side is going to be 'O for the wings of a dove' and other church music, but on the reverse side it is to be carols and there is always a big demand for them."

Robin was nearly crying.

"We didn't even come top in that talent contest, so now they've mucked up my record I've absolutely nothing to look forward to ever again."

"You are playing the piano for 'Ye Frog and Ye Crow'" Philip reminded him, "and it is still your swirled version."

Robin was scornful.

"That's what you think! I bet you'd never know it was swirled for I'll be made to play as soft as if it was a cat playing in case I spoil Ann's singing. Not even a cat playing, more like the whiskers on the end of a cat's paws."

Philip was afraid this might be true.

"I really am awfully sorry for you, old man, for I can imagine how you feel. As you know, swirled tunes are not my cup of tea but for your sake I hope you are allowed to be noisier than you expect."

What made life even more trying for Robin was that Ann either had not taken in how excited Mr. Push was about her singing or just didn't care. She spent the whole week-end going out with Audrey and when they were in the house, though they chattered their heads off, nobody heard the record mentioned.

"I do feel sorry for Robin and Nigs," Lydia told Gemma as they walked back from school. "They were so looking forward to making a really noisy record."

"I know," Gemma agreed. "But you can't argue with people like Mr. Push. So odd to be a person like Ann, she was much more interested in hearing about Audrey going to Switzerland to learn to be a ski instructor than all those simply gorgeous things Mr. Push was saying about her voice."

Lydia dismissed Ann with a gesture.

"She's always been like that. I must make Dad go and see Miss Arrowhead. With all this fuss about the record he's kept putting it off, but I've got to learn that dance for Gemma and Sisters. Miss Arrowhead as good as promised she'd teach me one. I'll just die if she doesn't."

As it turned out there was no need for Philip to see Miss Arrowhead for the next day, when Lydia arrived for her usual morning class, Miss Arrowhead called her to her.

"Sit down, Lydie. I have something to tell you."

Miss Arrowhead was sitting on one of the student's benches so Lydia sat beside her.

"You remember I told you there could be no new dances learnt this side of Christmas. Didn't you wonder why?"

"Of course I did for you had as good as promised I could dance on my pointes, and . . ."

Miss Arrowhead held up a hand to stop Lydia.

"I'm afraid you are not going to like what I am going to tell you, but you have to try and see it from my point of view. Seeing things from someone else's point of view is always a difficult thing to do and it's particularly hard for you, Lydie."

Lydia turned scared eyes to Miss Arrowhead.

"What are you going to tell me?"

"That I shall be away for four months. It's a great

honour. I have been chosen to adjudicate a dancing contest in South America."

Lydia had turned quite white.

"Four months! Then who is teaching me?"

Miss Arrowhead took one of Lydia's hands in hers.

"I've given the matter much thought and I have decided it would not help for you to go to a strange teacher

"What are you going to tell me?"

for four months, so I am entrusting you to Polly. I admit this means a great deal of repetition but that will do you no harm."

"But . . ." Lydia exploded.

Again Miss Arrowhead stopped her.

"I know you do not think Polly will teach you as well as I do, but she is very sound technically and I know will see that you work hard and don't get into bad habits."

Lydia was almost past speech but she managed to gasp:

"I won't learn with Polly. I won't."

Miss Arrowhead gave her a kiss.

"Don't be a silly child. Come on, we must get on with our lesson, there won't be many more as I leave this week-end. Now run along to the barre and let me see some pliés."

CHAPTER SIX

GLOOM

WHILE Lydia was talking to Miss Arrowhead Gemma was talking about Juliet with Mrs. Calvert.

"I do not know of course," Mrs. Calvert said, "what the university producer has in mind, but I believe in finding the character as we believe Juliet was meant to be and then build on that. It's the only way to play a character with roots, and a rootless character cannot live."

Gemma nodded.

"She's a difficult girl to understand. I mean I don't know any girls of just fourteen who fall in love like she did."

"You have to remember Juliet wasn't English, she was of Latin blood—a fiery little aristocrat living in Verona.

I think too her home was like a greenhouse—a place for forcing on young plants. Remember that scene we worked on between Juliet and her mother where her mother, talking about a possible marriage, said: 'I would say thou hadst suck'd wisdom from thy teat,' and remember too how her mother pointed out that girls younger than Juliet were not only married but already had babies."

"I suppose really I ought to be looking for a boy friend," Gemma suggested. "It would help me to understand just a little of how she felt."

Mrs. Calvert smiled.

"I doubt if any boy friend you could find in Headstone would help you to understand little Juliet's feeling for Romeo. In fact, though most people fall in love at some time in their lives—many several times—the sort of blind passion Juliet had for Romeo is experienced by very few. No, what you have to do is to act—to give the semblance of how Juliet felt. In ten years' time you will almost certainly act her better, but you will have lost what you now have to give, which is her extreme youth."

Being so deeply involved as she was with Juliet the surge of feeling washing through Trelawny Drive had more or less missed Gemma. She knew of course that she and Lydia were no longer required to sing for Robin's record. She knew dimly that Robin was furious at the new arrangement. She knew, for Ann told her so, that she had only agreed to sing the solo for Robin's record because otherwise the recording of St. Giles choir was off. But since Lydia had cried at the singing rehearsal she had heard no more of her troubles and had forgotten about them, so she was quite unprepared for the hysterical Lydia who joined her after school.

"What on earth's the matter?" she said staring at Lydia's white tear-stained face.

"I've been holding it in and holding it in until I can't hold it in any more. Oh, you can't guess the awful thing that's happened . . . you see . . ."

Gemma drew Lydia into a doorway and gave her a handkerchief to mop up her tears.

"Try and stop crying because I can't hear."

Lydia, after several false starts and through hiccupping sobs, poured out her story.

"Imagine four whole months when she thinks I'll work with Polly but I won't, I absolutely won't. I like Polly but she's no good teaching someone like me."

Except what she had learnt from Lydia Gemma knew nothing about dancing. But it was clear that Miss Arrowhead, who was not only a good but a conscientious teacher, would not leave Lydia to learn with her niece Polly if she thought it would do her any harm. However, it was no good saying anything like that to Lydia so instead she made a suggestion.

"Are you having a lesson tomorrow?"

"Yes. She doesn't fly to South America until the end of the week."

"Then ask her if you could have special lessons with Miss Lansdowne. They say she's good."

Miss Lansdowne taught ballet at the drama school.

"She is good," Lydia agreed, "but she teaches the Cecchetti method and I haven't learnt that."

"Then ask her if you can go to someone else. I know Polly's her niece but I'd bet she'd understand."

Lydia shook her head.

"She won't. She knows Polly can't teach me anything new but she says the repetition won't hurt me but it will . . ."

The word "will" was drowned in more tears. Once again Gemma tidied Lydia up. Privately she thought that from the sound of things Lydia was doomed to lessons with Polly but she still tried to cheer her up.

"Don't give up hope yet, even now Miss Arrowhead may change her mind and send you to learn with someone else while she's away."

"Oh dear!" Alice said to Philip that night. "I shall be glad when that wretched record is made and when Lydie has settled down to learn with Polly. This house is like a morgue."

"How true," Philip agreed. "I'm holding my thumbs that nothing happens to upset Gemma. All we need is to have her in one of her tantrums."

Luckily nothing else went wrong for any of the family but Lydia went about like a tragedy queen and she and Robin took out some of their misery by quarrelling with each other. Then a change of plan let a little light on the family gloom. It came in a telephone call from Barry Thomas to Philip.

"Eli Push is very rushed just now. He was wondering if Ann and, of course, Robin could come to the London recording studios on Saturday week."

In the end it was decided to take not only Ann and Robin to London but Nigs and Lydia. Gemma could have gone too but she said she would rather stay at home and work at Juliet.

"With you all away I'll have a gorgeous day acting Juliet all over the house."

"It's a heaven-sent arrangement," said Alice to Philip. "I'm going to blow the expense and take Lydie to a ballet matinée, there isn't a ballet at Covent Garden that week but there is a visiting company. Lydie seems to know all about them for she says they are fabulous."

Philip too had made plans.

"George Gamesome has offered to take Nigs and Robin sight-seeing so I'll take Ann to a concert. Then we'll all meet somewhere for an early supper and then George

Gamesome will drive us home. How's that for a day out?"

Everyone agreed it certainly would be a grand day.

"Of course I'm still sick as muck that my record is going to be spoilt by Ann," Robin told Nigs, "but I must say seeing the Chamber of Horrors does make up a bit."

"Are you thrilled about going to the ballet matinée?" Gemma asked Lydia.

Lydia gave a little skip which might have been expressing pleasure or excitement.

"It's the de Clara Ballet. The dancers are of all nationalities, they train in France somewhere. I've always and always wanted to see them for Miss Arrowhead told me Monsieur de Clara is the greatest teacher in the world."

"Does he still dance?"

"I think so, parts like Carabosse in 'The Sleeping Princess' and Coppelius in Coppélia, but it's the dancers he's trained who have made his ballet famous." A look of ecstasy came over Lydia's face. "Monsieur de Clara imagine!"

Something about Lydia made Gemma worry in case somehow the de Clara ballet let her down.

"I do hope you have a lovely time on Saturday."

Lydia, regardless of the fact that they were walking in a main road, turned three pirouettes.

"I will," she called out. "You wait and see."

CHAPTER SEVEN

YE FROG AND YE CROW

THE record company had offered to send a car for Ann and Robin but George Gamesome turned down the offer saying he would bring everybody up in his car.

"Though, mind you, I couldn't have done it if we had the drums," he told Robin and Nigs, "so maybe it's a good thing they aren't wanted."

In spite of the day in London and the Chamber of Horrors the wound was still too raw from what both boys considered Robin's ruined chances for the subject to be spoken of lightly, so they treated this remark with the silence it deserved.

The recording was at ten so the family made an incredibly early start. Gemma, in a dressing-gown, came down to wave them off.

"Oh darling," said Alice as she kissed her good-bye, "you will eat a good lunch, won't you, and don't wait up for I'm sure we shall be late back."

Gemma never minded being alone.

"Don't fuss. I'll be all right. Have a wonderful time, everybody."

"We will," the family shouted.

Gemma went back into the house to get her breakfast. She knew that she too was going to have an exciting day for the previous afternoon, just as she was changing to go home, Mrs. Calvert had sent for her.

"Oh Gemma," she had said, "the Dean has been on the phone. He wants me to bring you to tea at the university tomorrow. He will have John Cann there to meet us. If I call for you at 3.30 with the car can you be ready?"

Gemma had agreed she could be ready and added that it was a good day as the rest of the family would be in London. What she did not say was that she was not going to tell anybody about tea with the Dean for somehow she felt shy about meeting John Cann. Suppose he despised her as a little girl? She could never face jokes at home about meeting her Romeo.

The family arrived in London in splendid time and

after a second breakfast they drove to the recording studios.

Ann had not thought much about making the record. She had learnt the words of "Ye Frog and Ye Crow" and had, with Philip's help, fitted the words to Robin's swirled version of the tune. She had whispered to her father on the way to London that she did hope that there would not be too many repeats as she thought a little of "Ye Frog and Ye Crow" went a long way. She was not nervous because she did not know there was anything to be nervous about, and for once she was quite unselfconscious because she knew nobody would be watching her—only listening to her. She was therefore totally unprepared for the reception she received.

Eli Push believed that in Ann he had a real discovery. He was given to exaggeration but when he said she had the voice of the century he believed it. So he treated her as the voice of the century. Already the corridor leading to the studios was carpeted with that sort of carpet—and it was red—which makes you wonder if you have lost your feet, so he could not lay down any more, but he could and did stand on the doorstep to welcome Ann himself.

"Good-morning, good-morning, little lady. This is a great day in the life of my company. The day when we record for the first time the voice of our little nightingale." He handed Ann some expensive roses. "A few flowers to lay at your feet."

Ann was never good at replying to compliments but this fulsomeness reduced her to complete silence. Not so Nigs. He gave a hiccup and rushed back into the road where he could laugh in peace.

"Our little nightingale!" he groaned between spasms. "Our little nightingale!"

Lydia joined him looking scornful.

"Imagine calling Ann 'little lady'! It's the sort of thing she hates."

Robin put his head round the door.

"Pack it up, you two idiots. There's nothing to laugh about, Nigs. I told you it would be all Ann this morning."

Philip looked out.

"Come on Lydie and Nigs. We're going where we can listen. At least I am and you can if you behave yourselves. Cut along, Robin, just follow Mr. Push and Ann." Then he whispered: "Keep your chin up, after all you did swirl the music."

As Robin had feared the producer made him play very softly—not so softly as the hairs on the end of a cat's paws, as he had expected, but far too softly for swirled music which, in his opinion, needed plenty of noise.

"Mouse music," he thought. "That's what I'm playing —mouse music."

"Ye Frog and Ye Crow" was set to a pleasant but artless little tune. It was not really suitable for Ann's powerful voice, but she had the gift of sincerity so whatever she sang came over to the audience as if it mattered. This song had, too, a plaintive quality which suited her. It was about a crow who deceitfully urged a frog to come out of the water so that he might eat him. The poor frog believed the stories the crow told him so he swam out of the pond. On landing beside the crow he asked:

" 'But where is the sweet music on yonder green hill, O?
    And where are all the dancers, the dancers in yellow?
    All in yellow, all in yellow?' "

It finished on a broken line while the frog still asking questions, was swallowed.

After recording Robin waited until the light turned to green then he whispered to Ann:

"Playing like that absolutely ruined my swirl."

"Don't think about it," Ann advised. "Think of the simply gorgeous lunch Mr. Gamesome is going to give us as soon as we've finished here."

In the main hall an argument had developed.

"It was grand," Eli Push said, "but I still think for this first song of Ann's she should sing straight. Call an accompanist and we'll try that."

Philip was angry but he kept calm.

"There's no need to send for an accompanist. I am a professional musician and could accompany Ann if she needed anyone other than Robin."

Mr. Push did not like his plans interfered with.

"Well you accompany her then. I've a fancy she'll come over even better singing straight."

Philip turned to Barry Thomas.

"If I remember rightly you telephoned my house after that talent contest and asked Robin if his group would like to make a record."

Barry Thomas looked embarrassed.

"Well yes, but . . ."

"My children," Philip went on, "have been brought up to believe what is said to them. Robin believed and trusted you."

Eli Push was getting annoyed.

"What is all this about? I only said I wished to hear Ann sing the song straight."

Mr. Push might not have spoken for all the interest Philip took in what he had said. He went on talking to Barry Thomas.

"Then your plans changed and St. Giles choir became involved. Then the record became Ann's record instead of Robin's record. Now it is suggested that Robin and his swirled music shall be cut altogether. I won't have it. You may destroy my son's faith in human nature."

40

"I never heard such a pack of nonsense." said Eli Push, "just because I want the best from my little nightingale."

Suddenly George Gamesome—who had listened in amazement to Philip who he had not thought had it in him to make a fuss—decided to take a hand. He got up and sat down beside Eli Push.

"There's nothing to discuss. That contract her father signed for Ann was for three records, the first to be 'Ye Frog and Ye Crow' in the version composed by her brother and accompanied by him. If you want to change that you've broken your contract so we may as well be moving."

"Good gracious!" Robin said to Ann. "What are they doing out there? They've had time to play the recording back forty times. I'm dying of hunger."

"You better not think about food then," Ann advised, "for we're certain to have to do it again. Nothing is ever right the first time."

Ann was quite correct. A minute later the producer came back.

"That was fine," he said. "Now we'll do it again with a little more sound from you, Robin."

CHAPTER EIGHT

SWAN LAKE

BECAUSE Nigs and Lydia had heard the argument there was no point in trying to keep the news there had been one from Ann and Robin. The story—rather exaggerated by Nigs—was repeated two or three times and each time was received with rapture by Robin.

"Oh Dad, how smashing you standing up to him! Oh my goodness, I wish I'd heard you say that, Mr. Gamesome! I wondered why they let me play louder, now I know. I only wish I could have seen Mr. Push's face . . ."

When Ann got a chance to get a word in she said:

"You haven't told us yet how we sounded—the final recording I mean."

There was the slightest pause. The truth was, flushed with victory, nobody had been listening very carefully to the recordings. But Philip could not hear music without subconsciously registering how it sounded.

"I liked the last recording. It was your best, Ann, and we could hear you, Robin, it was clearly your swirled version of the song."

"Good!" said Robin. "I know you wish really it wasn't swirled, which makes it all the more gorgeous that you fought Mr. Push for my rights."

After such a long and exciting morning the family were ravenous for lunch. At the restaurant George Gamesome had selected there was a good table d'hôte menu and they all ate solidly through each course, starting with potted shrimps, melon or soup and finishing with the most splendid trolley on which were all the very best cakes, fruit and puddings. They had only just finished eating when Alice looked at her watch.

"Come on, Lydie. Time for your matinée."

This drew attention to something that in all the other excitements the family had missed. Lydia was carrying a carrier bag. As she got it out from under her chair Alice saw it.

"What's that for, darling?"

"Things," said Lydia in an off-putting voice. "My programme to take home and the spoon from my ice—if I get one in the interval. You know I collect ice spoons."

Seeing what Lydia had eaten for lunch the idea of her still hoping for an ice made them laugh.

"Greedy guts!" said Ann. "All the same I hope you enjoy the dancing."

Alice had decided to give Lydia a real treat so they had seats in the front row of the dress circle. The de Clara Ballet were more famous for reviving old classics than for commissioning new work. That afternoon they were dancing "Swan Lake". Lydia was determined her mother should enjoy herself, so though she had never seen the ballet as she knew the story and some of the choreography she insisted on telling it to her.

"Don't read that programme, Mum, I'll tell you."

"Do give me that silly old carrier," said Alice, "it will be in your way."

Lydia pushed the carrier under her seat.

"No it won't. Now listen. This is the story of a lot of girls who were turned into swans by a wicked magician called Rotbart—Miss Arrowhead says sometimes he looks like an owl and sometimes like a man."

"It just says 'Rotbart—a magician' here," said Alice peering at her programme.

"You don't see the swans except perhaps as flying birds in the first act. It's a party because Prince Siegfried is twenty-one. That's when his mother tells him he has got to choose a girl to marry at the next court ball."

"How do you tell a thing like that in dancing?" Alice asked.

Lydia was a little hazy about that but she was not going to say so.

"Gesture and mime. Well, that's most of what happens in the first act unless the swans fly over, but they don't always. Act 2 is gorgeous. It's by the lake and it's midnight so all the girls who were swans are being girls. They do some marvellous dancing but then one of the

43

Prince's men comes and tries to shoot them but the leading swan, who is called Odette, pleads with the Prince to spare them. Well of course Odette and Siegfried fall in love. He wants her to come to the ball but of course she can't because of having to be a swan again."

"Does Rotbart hear all this?"

"Oh yes, and Odette is very frightened of him and warns Siegfried that he will try and prevent them loving each other. Then the dawn comes and Odette and all the girls turn back into swans."

"I see the next scene is the court ball," said Alice.

"Yes, and Rotbart has dressed up his daughter, whose name is Odile, to pretend to be Odette and she deceives Siegfried."

"I don't wonder," said Alice, "seeing the same girl is dancing both parts."

Lydia nodded.

"Anyway it works and at the end of the act Prince Siegfried announces that he's going to marry the daughter of The Black Swan. That's what Rotbart is calling himself."

The orchestra was filing in. Alice laid a hand on one of Lydia's.

"Tell me the rest of the story in the first interval. I love Tchaikovsky so I don't want to miss a note."

For both Alice and Lydia it was an afternoon of pure enchantment. When the curtain finally fell Lydia was almost in tears.

"I can't bear it to end ever, ever, ever."

Between clapping Alice whispered:

"Cheer up, let's think of the day when I am sitting up here watching you dance Odette."

Lydia raised her head as if she had heard a distant trumpet call.

"Yes, let's think of that. I think absolutely anything is worth doing to make that happen. Don't you, Mum?"

44

Alice stood up.

"Don't forget your carrier and here's the programme to put in it. Now hold my hand, we mustn't lose each other."

Lydia and Alice were not the only ones to have enjoyed their afternoon. The boys had got hold of a guide in the Chamber of Horrors who had given them a most graphic description of the murder of a poor woman who had finished up being cut into small pieces and cooked.

"And some was fried, Mum, and some was boiled," Robin told Alice, but she interrupted him.

"I'm sorry, darling, but whatever happened to the poor lady I don't want to know about it while I'm eating tea."

The concert had been a great success too but had left Philip and Ann in an almost trance-like state.

George Gamesome, looking round, felt proud. It had not been an easy day to organize but here they all were safe and sound, full of tea and the car waiting for them just up the road. Not bad organization.

"Well, if you've eaten all you can I suggest we get going. Meet you all by those pot plants in the entrance in five minutes."

In five minutes George Gamesome was standing by the pot plants. He was joined almost at once by Philip, Nigs and Robin and soon afterwards by Alice and Ann.

"Now where's Lydie?" asked George Gamesome looking at his watch.

"She was with us a second ago," said Alice. "She must be just coming."

But Lydia was not just coming. And a quarter of an hour later she still had not come.

CHAPTER NINE

ROMEO

GEMMA, having cleared the table, slightly dusted the house and made her bed, had spent the morning deciding what to wear to meet John Cann. Her half of the wardrobe in the bedroom she shared with Ann was as usual bulging with clothes. As a rule she was clever with clothes but that day she found she hadn't an idea. How did you in your ordinary clothes make yourself look the sort of person Mrs. Calvert had described as a fiery little aristocrat? The trouble was, she decided as she tried on dress after dress before the long glass, that grown-up girls nowadays wore much the same clothes as schoolgirls. They even wore their hair the same way—it really was difficult.

In the end she decided on a green outfit with a matching coat. It was new and she always felt good in new clothes and it had a neckline that she thought gave her a sophisticated look.

Alice, knowing Gemma's powers as a cook, had left her a cold lunch. After she had eaten it and washed up and listened to a play on the radio it was time to dress and well before 3.30 she was on the doorstep waiting for Mrs. Calvert.

Mrs. Calvert was in her way as anxious about this meeting with Gemma's Romeo as Gemma was. She was very aware that she was not likely to have Gemma in her school for long. She was sure some good offer would turn up for her and her mother would insist that she accepted it. So it was a wonderful chance that the Dean had turned up looking for a Juliet. She was perfectly aware she would not only not be producing the play but would have very little officially to do with the production. But behind the scenes was a different matter. Whatever the producer wanted to do the Juliet Gemma gave him would be the Juliet she had moulded.

As Mrs. Calvert stopped her car outside the Robinsons' house in Trelawny Drive she looked with approval at Gemma. She really was a beautiful child, she thought, and that green outfit suited her perfectly.

"We're both punctual," she said leaning over to open her car door. "I'm glad for I thought if we were early we might manage to find a student who would show us the theatre before we go to the Dean's house."

"Haven't you ever seen it?" Gemma asked.

"Not empty. I saw it when the university was officially opened but, of course, it didn't even feel like a theatre that day."

They were lucky, they found a girl student apparently at a loose end who was quite willing to show them the theatre.

"It's a queer sort of place," the girl said. "It has no curtains or anything but it's good for debates and when there was that Vietnam march last year lots of us locked ourselves in there before the march—it was rather fun though we got sick of living on sandwiches."

Mrs. Calvert thanked the girl and said they would find their own way out. They stood in one of the aisles and looked round. The stage was on ground level and the seats rose above it tier after tier. At the back of the stage there was a rostrum and above that two galleries. Mrs. Calvert's nostrils were flaring as if she could smell something good.

"Look at that rostrum and those galleries. What wonderful use the producer can make of those. Imagine the fights between the Montagues and Capulets—and the processions! Lucky fellow, he will have fun."

Gemma was of course seeing herself as Juliet.

"Do you think it's difficult with no curtain, I mean about getting on and off?"

"I'm sure it isn't. I imagine this shaped theatre is the theatre of the future so it's a good thing you should get used to them. I belong to the days of an orchestra pit and a stage of which the curtain was the fourth wall. I loved it and I like chandeliers and gilt and red plush. . . . I find all this unrelieved concrete rather hard to take but you won't."

The Dean's house was a pleasant red brick Edwardian building.

"Fortunately for me," said the Dean as he greeted them, "this house was already here so it seemed a waste of money to pull it down. But I fancy most of the faculty are ashamed of it."

The Dean led the way up to his study on the first floor.

"The drawing-room is on the ground floor," he explained, "but my wife is entertaining some local ladies so I thought we would do better on our own. John Cann is here."

John Cann was an impressive-looking young man. He had almost black hair and deep-set dark blue eyes. He was over six foot high and so thin he was almost gaunt. He was standing looking out of the window when Mrs. Calvert and Gemma arrived, but he came forward to meet them with a shy, charming smile.

The Dean led Mrs. Calvert to the tea table and asked her to pour out. John and Gemma, having been given cups of tea and some sandwiches, sat down on the cushioned window ledge.

"Have you studied the whole of Romeo yet?" Gemma asked.

John spoke with such eagerness it was as if something was boiling inside him, waiting to pour out.

"Sort of. I don't see him as all romantic. I think he

was very earthy and human. I think that's why Juliet, used to so much artificiality, fell for him as she did. How do you see him?"

"I haven't thought much about Romeo," Gemma admitted truthfully, "but I can see that might be a reason —yes it might. I have often thought that Romeo was like a gigantic wind, there was nothing once she had met him that Juliet could do to prevent him blowing her away."

"Nothing either of them could do," said John. Then he quoted:

> " 'O, speak again, bright angel! for thou art
> As glorious to this night, being o'er my head,
> As is a winged messenger of heaven
> Unto the white-upturned wondering eyes
> Of mortals that fall back to gaze on him
> When he bestrides the lazy-pacing clouds
> And sails upon the bosom of the air.' "

Gemma picked up her cue.

> " 'O Romeo, Romeo! wherefore art thou Romeo?
> Deny thy father, and refuse thy name;
> Or, if thou wilt not, be but sworn my love,
> And I'll no longer be a Capulet.' "

The Dean and Mrs. Calvert had stopped talking and were smiling at Gemma and John.

"Started already," said the Dean, "but leave that until rehearsals start. Come and have some more to eat."

Of course Gemma and John did not stop quoting, indeed after tea they ran through the whole of the balcony scene. At the end Gemma said to John:

"You're going to be marvellous."

John squeezed her arm.

"We'll both be marvellous," he said.

"Well, that was very pleasant," said Mrs. Calvert as

she and Gemma got into the car to go home. "What do you think of him?"

Gemma hadn't the words to explain how strange John had made her feel.

"Oh, he's good, awfully good."

"You'll look well together," said Mrs. Calvert. "He so tall and dark and you so fair." Then she had an idea. "My husband is out, do you think your aunt would let me take you back to supper with me?"

Gemma explained where the cousins were.

"So I could come and I'd love to. But I must leave a note saying where I am in case they get back before I do."

At the house Gemma went into the kitchen and left a note on the kitchen table knowing her aunt would be certain to put the kettle on for a cup of tea as soon as she got in. She went back into the hall and was just leaving the house when the telephone rang. She was in half a mind not to answer for it wouldn't be for her, but her uncle expected whoever was handy to answer the phone. She picked up the receiver.

"Hullo!"

It was Alice on the other end.

"Oh Gemma! I was afraid you were out. Has Lydie telephoned?"

"Lydie! Of course not. Why should she?"

Alice sounded near breaking point.

"She's missing. Your uncle's with the police now. I don't know what we're going to do. Please stay by the phone."

50

CHAPTER TEN

WHERE IS LYDIE?

WHEN Gemma told her what had happened Mrs. Calvert took command.

"Your aunt is sure to telephone again in case Lydie has phoned here. When she rings tell her that I am here and will stay here until Lydie's found."

"If only Lydie could telephone," said Gemma. "But if she's been kidnapped I suppose she can't."

Mrs. Calvert dismissed that.

"Don't let's suppose anything so awful. In a large restaurant it's so easy to miss people. Then finding herself lost the child might have panicked and run out into the street."

Gemma looked at Mrs. Calvert in surprise.

"I can't see Lydie panicking. I think she would go up to the first person on the staff she saw and say 'I'm lost'."

"Let's hope that has happened in which case we should hear good news soon. Meanwhile I shall put hot water bottles in the beds and some soup on, I'm sure they will all be tired and cold when they get in."

Gemma sat by the telephone feeling desperate. What had happened to Lydie? You read such awful things in the papers about children lured away by strangers. But Lydie would never go off with a stranger, they had all had it dinned into them over and over again how dangerous that could be. But if Lydie hadn't been kidnapped where was she? From what Aunt Alice had said it sounded as if she had been missing a long while. If she had not Uncle Philip would not have gone to the police.

It seemed to Gemma she had been sitting by the telephone for hours when at last it rang. It was Philip on the line.

"Gemma? Any news?"

"No, but Mrs. Calvert is here, she says she will stay until Lydie's found, and she's seeing to things like hot water bottles and soup."

"Bless her!" said Philip. "Now listen, George Gamesome is bringing Ann and Robin back—they've already gone. Your aunt and I are at the Police Station. Take down the number because they must be told at once if Lydie rings." ~

Gemma wrote down the number.

"I'll ring. I'm sitting beside the telephone."

"Good. The police seem to think Lydie might have slipped off deliberately somewhere. There are uniformed men on the doors and they swear they would have spotted a scared child, or one being forcibly taken away. But if that's true where on earth would Lydie go and why?"

Suddenly Gemma remembered that day when she had walked home from school with Lydia in tears. "Imagine four whole months when she thinks I'll work with Polly, but I won't, I absolutely won't . . ."

"I suppose," she said tentatively, "she couldn't have gone to anyone who teaches dancing? I mean, you know how she hates learning with Polly."

There was silence on the line, then when Philip spoke there was a tinge of hope in his voice.

"Dancing! That's an idea. I'll tell the police at once."

"She did have a paper carrier when she left," said Gemma. "I wondered what it was for but I suppose it could have held her shoes."

"Her dancing shoes!" Philip gasped. "Of course it could. Clever girl! I must go and tell the police."

About an hour later George Gamesome brought Ann and Robin home. He was enormously relieved to find

52

Mrs. Calvert in charge for he had been afraid he would have to take over.

"Extraordinary business," he told Mrs. Calvert. "One moment the girl was there and the next moment she was gone."

Robin and Nigs thought far too much fuss was being made but if there was going to be an uproar then they wanted to be in the middle of the excitement, not dragged home to Headstone.

"She'll turn up," Robin said confidently. "You know Lydie, she can look after herself."

Mrs. Calvert shooed him into the kitchen.

"Let's hope you are right. Now come and have some soup and then bed. Does he want soup too?" she looked at Nigs.

"No, thank you." George Gamesome shepherded Nigs out of the front door. "We must get home. Let us know when there's any news."

Ann was looking terribly white and tired Gemma thought.

"Wouldn't you like some soup?" she asked.

Ann shook her head.

"I'm so scared, Gemma. I keep thinking and thinking suppose she's been murdered."

"I wouldn't think that," said Gemma firmly. "I think she's gone to get someone to teach her to dance—you know how she hates learning with Polly."

Ann shook her head.

"What good would that do? She couldn't go to London to learn."

"Well, you know Lydie—if she wants something she just wants it, she doesn't see difficulties."

But Ann did not hear her. Worn out by the long day and the anxiety she slid to the floor in a faint.

Ann soon came round and was helped by Mrs. Calvert

into an armchair in the living-room, where soup was spooned into her mouth.

Robin joined Gemma by the telephone.

"Fancy Ann fainting!" he said. "I couldn't imagine her doing that."

Gemma felt she had better keep off the subject of Lydia.

"How did the recording go?"

Robin sat on the bottom step of the stairs.

"Goodness, it's so long ago I'd forgotten that. It was smashing. Dad told Mr. Push off and I was allowed to play loud enough for my swirling to be heard. Imagine, if Dad hadn't told him off he was going to let Ann sing the song straight. I wouldn't have even been playing the piano."

In spite of her anxiety Gemma was impressed.

"Told Mr. Push off! How awfully brave."

"Wasn't it? Nigs told me it was gorgeous hearing him do it."

The telephone bell rang. Ann and Mrs. Calvert came to the sitting-room door, even Robin came closer to listen. It was Philip on the phone.

"Lydie has been found. The police have her. We shall stay in London tonight and come home by train tomorrow morning."

Robin turned and stumped up the stairs.

"I always said there was no need to flap and you see I was perfectly right."

CHAPTER ELEVEN

LYDIA'S STORY

A VERY subdued Lydia came back to Trelawny Drive the next morning.

The journey back to Headstone had passed in almost complete silence. Not because Alice and Philip had sent Lydia to Coventry but because both were struggling to think of a way to bring home to Lydia how dreadful her behaviour had been. Punishments were not things the

"I always said there was no need to flap."

Robinsons went in for if they could help it, but if there had to be one it had to fit the crime. What punishment would bring home to Lydia the appalling suffering she had caused?

They had travelled on an early train so when Philip, Alice and Lydia arrived at the house Ann and Robin had already left to join their choirs. Gemma was in her room studying Juliet and nursing a cold she had suddenly started. She came to the top of the stairs to greet the family. She tried to sound natural.

"Hullo, everybody! Nice you're back. I can't kiss you, Aunt Alice, I've got a very sneezy cold."

"Poor pet!" said Alice. "Ought you to be in bed?"

"No. I think it's the quick sort, it doesn't feel too bad."

Alice's mind was clearly not on Gemma's cold.

"Well you better stay in today."

Philip turned to Lydia.

"Go up to your room and go to bed. I'll come and talk to you after lunch."

"Are you coming to church, Philip?" Alice asked.

Philip nodded.

"Of course."

Gemma went back to Juliet. Presently she heard the front door shut and from the window she saw Alice and Philip hurrying up the road. She wondered about Lydia. Uncle Philip hadn't said nobody was to speak to her. But from the way he spoke it was clear she was in terrible disgrace.

"Poor little beast!" thought Gemma. "Of course it was very wrong to go off on her own. Still, I hate to think of her up there all alone, most likely crying. I'll just see if she wants anything."

Lydia's room was a converted boxroom reached by a ladder. Gemma stood at the bottom of the ladder and called up to it.

"Lydie! Lydie! It's me, Gemma. They've gone to church. Do you want anything?"

The door opened and Lydia looked out. Not at all tear-stained but defiant.

"They can shut me up as long as they like but I'm not a bit sorry. It was something I'll remember always."

"What happened to you? We were worried to death."

Lydia sat down on the floor, her feet on the top rung of the ladder.

"I wouldn't mind some biscuits or some cake but first I'll tell you about yesterday."

Gemma sat down at the bottom of the ladder.

"Go on."

"Well, you know I said I wouldn't work with Polly. Then Mum said she would take me to see the de Clara Ballet. Oh Gemma, he's the best teacher in the world. I can't tell you how glorious the dancing was in 'Swan Lake'."

"You didn't try to see him, did you?"

Lydia looked exalted.

"I didn't just try to see him. I did see him. I had it all planned before we went to London. My shoes were in my carrier bag and after tea I just slipped out and got in a taxi."

"Where did you get the money?"

"I've been saving my pocket money—but actually the taxi cost more than I thought it would so I hadn't enough left to telephone you. I truly had meant to do that so no one would fuss. I knew Dad or Mum would be sure to ring here."

"Go on," Gemma urged. "What did you do when you got to the theatre?"

"Well, I went round to the back where I knew the stage door would be like it was that time we did a Gemma and Sisters in a proper theatre. I found it quite easily. There was a light over the door and the words 'Stage door'. Inside a man was sitting who looked at everybody as they came in."

"The stage doorkeeper," said Gemma, who had gone behind many times when she had lived with her mother.

Lydia leant forward.

"I didn't know what to do. You see, I had thought with an enormous ballet the man wouldn't know everybody and I could squeeze in. But the ballet were all inside, I think they must have supper in the theatre. Then a woman came out with a little poodle. She put the poodle down to walk but she stayed and talked to the doorman."

Evidently Lydia had reached a point in the story where she was not sure of approval for she licked her lips and looked furtive.

"Go on," said Gemma. "What about the poodle?"

"Well, it was awfully sweet and very, very tiny so I picked it up just to kiss it . . ."

Gemma showed signs of getting up.

"If you make the story up I'll go back to my room."

"Oh very well. It wasn't just because it was sweet, I carried it round the corner so the woman would think it was lost."

"And did she?"

"My goodness, did she! She ran up and down screaming 'Minou! Minou!' Then the doorman came out and so did some other men. But they couldn't find her because I was in a door and I had my hand over her mouth so she couldn't bark."

"How mean," said Gemma. "I bet she was frightened."

"I don't truly think she was because I never stopped stroking her and kissing her. And then I read what was on her collar."

"What?"

"Miss Minou de Clara! His very own dog. Well after

that it was easy. I brought Minou back to the theatre and everybody made a great fuss because I said I'd found her. Then Mr. de Clara came out and he asked me to come into his dressing-room."

"And then?" asked Gemma.

"After a little it was terrible for when I said I was a dancer he stopped being nice and saying 'thank you', instead he said 'I don't think Minou was lost at all. I think you stole her to get a chance to see me'."

"Oh, my goodness! " said Gemma. "What did you do?"

"I sat down and put on my shoes and without his asking I danced—exercises it was, well there wasn't much room for me. After a bit he stopped being angry and I could feel he was interested because he asked who taught me. So then I told him everything, about learning with Polly and seeing the matinée and how I had sneaked out after tea."

"And he said he'd teach you?"

Lydia shook her head.

"At first it was all fuss. Somebody was sent to ring the police to say where I was. Then somebody took my name and address. But just before I went away with the police lady, who came for me, he said—Monsieur de Clara his very own self said: 'I could not judge by the little I have seen but I think perhaps there is real talent. Learn for four months with this Polly. Repetition is good. One day I will send for you for an audition. Then we shall see'."

Lydia's voice faded away as she recalled the glorious words.

"So I suppose you think it was worth it?" said Gemma.

"Suppose it was you and your one chance to act before somebody great wouldn't you think it was worth it?"

Gemma got up.

"I'll get you some biscuits and milk."

What could she say? She remembered the agony in

Alice's voice as she had said "Lydie's missing". Could any result that might come from Lydie meeting Monsieur de Clara be worth the suffering she had caused? And yet in itself Lydie's driving ambition was a good thing. You could not get far without it. Oh, dear, how puzzling life was!

CHAPTER TWELVE

THE PUNISHMENT

PHILIP and Alice had a serious talk that afternoon on the best way to bring home to Lydia how cruelly thoughtless her behaviour had been.

"The trouble is," Alice pointed out, "Lydie believes—truly believes—that anything which is good for her dancing is a right thing to do."

"Granted that may be true," Philip agreed, "but she's got imagination, she should have guessed what agony we should go through when we found she was missing."

"If her money had held out she was going to telephone Gemma," Alice reminded him.

"But as we now know, that might have been no good for it was only by seconds that Gemma happened to be in for your call."

"What she could have done," said Alice, "only the silly child never thought of it, was to tell Robin where she was going. He wouldn't have told us a minute before he had to."

"I suppose she was afraid we'd come after her before she had a chance of seeing this man de Clara. Anyway I gather he told her off pretty thoroughly."

"But promised her an audition later on," Alice reminded him.

"And what good will that do? I thought he trained his dancers in France."

"I don't know whether it's France or London but either of course is out of the question for Lydie," Alice agreed, giving at the same time a small sigh as she thought of the scenes ahead when Lydia was invited to an audition she could not attend.

"What we have to find," said Philip, "is a punishment that really hurts. I don't think anything else is going to bring home to her how much suffering she caused us."

Alice looked shocked.

"You don't mean you'd beat her?"

"Of course not. When have I ever beaten the children? No, what I have in mind is Gemma and Sisters. I suggest we ask Rosie to take Lydie's place in all the Christmas performances."

Rosie Glesse was a pleasant little girl of Lydia's age. She was an exceptionally uninspired dancer but her ambitious mother believed her to be a genius. Rosie had taken Lydia's place in the months while she had an injured hip. They had all got on well with Rosie but had found Mrs. Glesse a great trial. Now, at the thought of replacing Lydia with Rosie, Alice gave a gasp.

"Oh, what a terrible punishment! Must we do that? It will ruin Lydia's Christmas, she'll be dreadfully unhappy."

"Can you think of anything else that will bring what she did home to her?"

Alice closed her eyes and recalled with a shudder last night. The dreadful fears that she couldn't hold back. The obvious concern of the police. The time spent waiting in the Police Station which had felt like hours.

"I suppose not. But I wish there was some other way. It's going to hurt all of us, it won't be half so much fun without Lydie."

Philip went up to Lydia's room to tell her what had been decided. She was lying on her bed reading the programme of the de Clara Ballet right the way through, advertisements and all, trying to recapture the magic of yesterday. She sat up when Philip came in.

"Hullo, Daddy! Can I come down now?"

Philip sat on the side of her bed.

"Mum and I have been talking about you. You have to be punished you know."

Lydia nodded.

"Truly I'm awfully sorry you and Mum got in a state but . . ."

"There aren't any 'buts', Lydia. We got in more than a state, you can imagine the dreadful things we thought might have happened to you."

"Kidnapped and murdered," Lydia suggested.

"Mum and I think that the punishment for making other people suffer is to suffer yourself. So we have decided that for all the Gemma and Sisters shows this Christmas we shall ask Rosie Glesse to take your place."

There was a stunned silence. In her worst imaginings Lydia had thought of nothing so awful as that. Four months without Miss Arrowhead was terrible but at least she and Polly could have worked at the national dances for Gemma and Sisters. No Gemma and Sisters at all! Dad couldn't mean it. He couldn't be so cruel . . . Lydia was so upset her voice became a whisper.

"Rosie will be terrible. She dances worse not better."

Philip got up.

"That's our bad luck. Come down when you feel like it. We will say no more about yesterday. You know your punishment and that is the end of the matter."

Lydia gazed at the door as it shut behind her father. Then she rolled over on her face and cried and cried. At first she told herself it was mean and unfair, all she had done was to try and get some good dancing lessons. Then gradually she remembered some of the things Robin had told her about yesterday. "A policewoman took Mum away and I think she was sick. She looked terrible." "Dad was green and white in stripes." It was wicked of her to have hurt them like that—she just hadn't thought. So now they were going to hurt her. No Gemma and Sisters! No Gemma and Sisters at all! It was unbearable.

Alice telephoned Mrs. Glesse who was charmed to be asked if Rosie could again take part in Gemma and Sisters.

"And this year," she said, "Rosie has a little dance on her pointes which Polly taught her. I'm sure that will go down well."

"I'm sure it will," thought Alice miserably as she put down the receiver, "but it will also rub salt in poor Lydie's wounds. She had so hoped to dance on her pointes this year."

The family, when they heard what Lydia's punishment was to be, were shocked.

"Poor Lydie! I call that tough," said Ann, "and it will hurt us too for we shall miss her awfully."

Robin told the news to Nigs.

"I think it's a terrible punishment," he said, "but actually it won't hurt us too much for Rosie, though she's dull, sings better than Lydie."

Nigs was full of sympathy.

"Poor old Lydie! What a beastly shame! Dad said he'd have beaten her if she was his daughter. I bet she'd rather have had that than miss Gemma and Sisters."

Robin nodded.

"I bet she would. It's lucky the Chamber of Horrors was so good—and the food of course—otherwise that day in London was a wash-out."

Gemma was desperately sorry for Lydia. She knew, for

she heard about it on their walks home from school, how unhappy Lydia was.

"And you see, Gemma, I didn't mean to be bad. Truly I just hoped Monsieur de Clara would say he would teach me. I never thought about anything else."

Gemma could only squeeze Lydia's hand and make sympathetic noises. But she did make one promise.

"When you hear about the audition wherever it is I will pay your fare, that is if you are allowed to go, for this time you must let everybody know where you're going."

Lydia was faintly cheered by Gemma's promise. It was a ray of light in a dark world.

"Thank you very much, Gemma. I'll keep remembering your promise. And you needn't worry about me saying where I've gone. I'll never, never make that mistake again—not so long as I live."

CHAPTER THIRTEEN

ANDREW HERON

GEMMA was asked to go to the university to meet the young man engaged to produce "Romeo and Juliet". Mrs. Calvert took her in her car. They had been asked to go straight to the theatre where they found a very different scene from the last time they were there.

The university had a strong drama group and they were all present. A few were to be auditioned for small parts but the majority were to be crowds, so when Mrs. Calvert and Gemma arrived they were being told whether they were to be members of the Capulet or Montague families, citizens of Verona, maskers, guards, watchmen or servants.

The producer, called Andrew Heron, was a quiet, vivid-looking man with evidently a strong personality for he was controlling everybody without apparent difficulty.

"As there are plenty of you," he told the students, "I don't propose to use any of you in two capacities. This means one costume apiece, which simplifies the wardrobe problem and the dressing situation. But, as I intend to make much use of crowds, when I want any of you to double it will be by adding something to your original costume."

"Do you suppose," Gemma whispered to Mrs. Calvert, "that Romeo and I will only have one costume each?"

"Could be," said Mrs. Calvert. "You never know what these modern producers will get up to."

"Now," said the producer, "will everybody leave the stage except those I have said should be Capulets."

There was a good deal of scuffling and arguing for evidently everybody did not remember what they had been told. But at last only about sixty men and twelve girls were left on the stage. These were told to give their names to the stage manager.

Once the Capulets were sorted out the same plan was carried out, first with the Montagues, then with citizens of Verona and finally with the other extras.

"Now," Andrew Heron called through his megaphone, "if all you crowds will either sit down and keep quiet or go I would like the principals on the stage."

Most of the crowd evidently wanted to see the principals for few left and after a preliminary clatter they were all seated.

Gemma was wearing the same outfit she had worn to meet John Cann.

"Give me your coat," said Mrs. Calvert. "Find John Cann, he will introduce you to the producer."

Gemma for once felt a little shy as she walked up an aisle and climbed the few steps on to the stage. The stage manager saw her. He was an eager-beaver young man determined to make his mark.

"I don't recognize you. Who are you playing?"

Gemma was glad to find someone in authority.

"I'm Gemma Bow. I'm to be Juliet."

The young man turned a deep crimson.

"Oh I say—I am a clot—of course I saw you in all your films when I was a kid . . ."

"Is John Cann here?" Gemma asked. "I know him."

"Not yet. But I think all the others are. You see that fat girl over there, she's the nurse. And that girl with the long black hair she's Lady Capulet, and that tall type she's talking to is Capulet. All of them were in 'Hamlet', the one who is Lady Capulet was Gertrude. I thought she was marvellous."

Gemma looked at the dark girl. She was about nineteen, she guessed, and very good-looking—not pretty exactly, more handsome. She wondered why, if she was a good enough actress to play Gertrude, they hadn't given her the part of Juliet.

The dark girl suddenly became conscious that someone's eyes were on her. She swung round and gave Gemma a long, queer look then, raising her voice, she came across the stage.

"Look who is here!! The great Gemma Bow stooping to act with us amateurs. Ought I to curtsey?"

Without Gemma seeing him John Cann had come on to the stage. He stood beside her.

"Yes, this is Gemma Bow. Gemma, meet Dulcie Culpepper." Then he grinned at Dulcie. "What was all that about? Gemma hasn't asked for special treatment. You aren't a queen now, you know."

Andrew Heron had seen John Cann arrive. He came over to him.

"Hullo, John!" Then he looked at Gemma. "And this

66

must be my Juliet. I'm Andrew Heron. Take her round and introduce her," he told John. "I've only two or three minor castings to do and then perhaps we could get away somewhere."

"My room," John suggested. "I've got some sherry."

"Mrs. Calvert's here," said Gemma.

John looked pleased.

"Good. Then she can hear about rehearsals."

John led Gemma round introducing her and explaining who she was and that she was playing Juliet. All the cast seemed willing to be friendly, for which Gemma was glad, for if they had behaved like Dulcie the going could have been tough.

After she had met the cast Gemma and John went to join Mrs. Calvert at the back of the theatre. On the way Gemma said :

"Did that Dulcie Culpepper girl want to play Juliet?"

"I expect she thought she ought to," John agreed. "But she couldn't have." He lowered his voice to a whisper. "She was terrible as Gertrude. All the critics who knew anything about Shakespeare said things like: 'Dulcie Culpepper was miscast' or else they didn't mention her at all. But some people—the ones who didn't know—thought she was fine for she looked wonderful and was very dramatic, only you could tell she was not thinking, just spouting."

"I see," said Gemma. "I must be careful to be extra polite to her. But I should think she'd be very good as Lady Capulet."

John had an infectious giggle which burst from him.

"I'd describe it as perfect casting."

Gemma giggled too, she couldn't help it.

The talk about the play in John's room was exciting for Andrew had produced the play before with a partly professional cast but with student extras.

"This stage is better," he told them, "because of the galleries but as well I'm going to use the body of the theatre so I can bring my crowds on from all directions. I am a great believer in speed."

"Not at the expense of the poetry I hope," said Mrs. Calvert.

Andrew hesitated.

"No. Of course there must be time for the music of the words to come through, but this is a young play and young people are always in a hurry. I must think of that too."

"It's because of speed that you are having no changes either of scenery or clothes, isn't it?" John asked.

"There will be changes of scenery of course," Andrew explained, "but all in front of the audience by a team who do nothing else, they'll be dressed as citizens of Verona."

"Do you mean to say Juliet is to wear one dress throughout?" Mrs. Calvert asked.

"I've got a brilliant designer," Andrew explained. "What she is working on for Juliet and Romeo and characters like the Capulets is a basic garment with various over garments. This will give the same effect as different dresses. For instance, in the balcony scene Juliet will wear just the basic garment, which will be white and flowing."

When it was time for them to leave Mrs. Calvert asked about rehearsals.

"I'm starting next week," Andrew explained, "but at first I'm only using my crowd. Full rehearsals should start in about a month. They will largely be at the week-ends."

Mrs. Calvert got up to go.

"Would you mind," she suggested casually, "if John came to me so the two can get used to working together?"

Andrew hesitated.

"Well, I suppose that wouldn't hurt. Anyway I can

change anything I don't like when the time comes."

In the car driving home Mrs. Calvert was very cock-a-hoop.

"If John works with me for a month I'll see speed doesn't ruin the play. So that disposes of our only worry."

Gemma thought of Dulcie.

"I hope you're right," she said.

CHAPTER FOURTEEN

ROSIE

ST. GILES choir were very busy working at the music for their recording. At first both Robin and Nigs found the extra practices a bore, then one day Mr. Reynolds, the choirmaster, told the choir some news that from the boys' point of view entirely changed the situation.

"We have decided that you shall all in a small way participate in any money this record may make. So much for each man, so much for each chorister and, of course, a special rate for soloists."

"My goodness," Robin told Nigs after school, "if only this record would be a best seller think of all the money I'll make! Enough to buy a honky-tonk piano."

"I always told you that you would," said Nigs. "I told you about the record of the boy singing 'O for the wings of a dove' that sold simply millions."

"Imagine," Robin gloated, "getting rich at my age! If only that awful 'Ye Frog and Ye Crow' catches on when I'm grown up I can just sit back and swirl tunes. I'll never have to do what they call 'an honest day's work'."

To save hurting Lydia it was planned to have the first

rehearsal of Gemma and Sisters at Nigs' house, but Lydia when she heard was furious.

"All right, so I'm being punished," she told her father. "But if you think I'm going to cry every time Rosie Glesse comes to a rehearsal you've another think coming. As a matter of fact, if you want to know, I was thinking of teaching Rosie the tap dance because Gemma never will, she thinks of nothing but Juliet."

Philip was impressed.

"That's very generous of you, darling."

Rosie Glesse, though overjoyed to be once again taking part in Gemma and Sisters, was secretly worried. Why was Lydia out of the show again? It couldn't be because Miss Arrowhead was away for she must know lots of dances for Gemma and Sisters she had danced in other years.

Rosie and Lydia never met at the dancing school for Lydia had her private lessons first thing in the morning, and though Lydia came to a general lesson on Saturday mornings it was the advanced class, which was outside Rosie's abilities. But Rosie was determined to meet Lydia before the first rehearsal. Something horrible might have happened, like Dad offering some enormous sum to a charity if she could dance in Lydia's place. It could have happened because Mum had been carrying on about how her talent wasn't recognized in the town.

Rosie's Saturday class finished at eleven o'clock and either her mother or father picked her up afterwards in the car. That week she invented an excuse.

"I've got to stay on to watch the advanced so could you fetch me at half-past twelve?"

"I can't believe anybody is more advanced than my Rosie," said Mrs. Glesse, "but twelve-thirty it is."

Because Monsieur de Clara had said four months repetition would do her no harm Lydia was really trying to work well with Polly. It was not much of a success because secretly she did not think Polly could teach her anything so she took criticism badly, but at least there were no rows.

As Rosie had hoped Lydia was at the advanced class so, having obtained permission to watch, she sat down beside her.

"Could I talk to you afterwards?"

Lydia might have agreed, but to teach Rosie the tap dance was one thing, it did not mean she was liking her much. She sounded as if that was how she felt.

"What about?"

Rosie was apologetic.

"Well, I can't tell you now exactly but if you could manage afterwards."

Lydia ungraciously agreed she might manage five minutes afterwards then, since anybody—even Rosie Glesse as audience—brightened the dreariness of a class taken by Polly she showed off, in fact she danced better than she had since Miss Arrowhead left.

"Thank goodness," thought poor Polly, "she's settling down."

Lydia had her reward in Rosie's unrestrained admiration.

"Oh Lydia, how glorious to dance like you! How I wish I could."

Lydia couldn't answer that since poor Rosie really was a terribly wooden dancer. So instead she said:

"What did you want to talk to me about?"

Rosie took a deep breath for what she had to say was awkward.

"Well, you know my Mum is always wanting me to dance at bazaars and things but people don't ask me. Lately she's been creating terribly and I thought perhaps Dad—you know, to help Mum—well perhaps Dad had offered to give a lot of money to charity if I could be in Gemma and Sisters—well he might have."

Lydia was thinking hard. Evidently no one had told the Glesses why Rosie was to take her place. Could she pretend she had stood down to help a charity? It would make her look like a saint. Then a better answer came to her. She would tell Rosie, under a vow of secrecy, part of the truth.

"No, it's not that at all. You see, we went to London because Ann and Robin were making a record and I decided . . ."

Rosie was a wonderful audience for she believed everything she heard, even the end of the story as Lydia now told it.

"And Monsieur de Clara said: 'You have genius, my child. It is my dearest wish to have you as my pupil. One day you will be my leading dancer, I swear it."

"Oh Lydie, how glorious! I think if he had said that to me I should have fainted dead away."

"I nearly did," said Lydia, by now believing every word she was saying, "but I knew Mum would worry so I said I must go. Then, Rosie, guess what happened—he kissed my hand."

Rosie was thrilled.

"If he'd kissed mine I wouldn't have washed it for days and days."

Lydia realised she must return to facts.

"Well, Mum was so worried I was lost Dad said I must be punished. So not being in Gemma and Sisters is my punishment."

"What a shame!" said Rosie. "You'd think they'd be proud with Monsieur de Clara saying those lovely things."

"Well actually they don't know all he said—only you know that and you must swear never, never to tell anybody. So you needn't worry about Gemma and Sisters because if you weren't being me somebody else would be."

Rosie heaved a sigh of relief.

"Oh good! But you do see I simply had to know before I went to a rehearsal, and you do see why I'm embarrassed to dance instead of you."

That gave Lydia an idea.

CHAPTER FIFTEEN

SONG REHEARSAL

ANN was increasingly happy at the Comprehensive. She was lucky at the start of the new school year in her teachers, they were so good she found herself looking forward to each new day for it was like diving into the deep sea to bring up treasures. She was understanding too that learning is limitless, that she could go on learning for ever. It was a glorious thought.

Ann became so tied to her books that she had begun to resent outside claims on her time. She still sang in the school choir but this term she was longing for an excuse to give it up. The difficulty was that as a leader and soloist she brought in a lot of House marks. As she was no good at games or gym these were the only House marks she did earn and so, if she stopped singing in the choir, it would be decidedly unpopular.

As usual when she had a problem she took it to her father. It was Sunday afternoon and he was reading "The Observer" after lunch.

"Hullo!" he said, putting down his paper. "Washing up finished?"

Ann sat on a stool at his feet and told him her problem.

"Honestly, with the church choir, it's a bit much and I can't give up the church choir because truthfully, without being conceited, I don't see what they'd do without me."

"I suppose these House marks are important?"

"I used to think they were but honestly now I don't really care which House wins."

Philip thought about that.

"Only you can decide the answer but since you've asked for my advice I'll give it to you. No one I think has the right to live entirely for themselves."

Ann was shocked.

"Of course not but I don't. I mean you know I do my share at home—really more than my share Gemma being Gemma—and there's the church choir and Gemma and Sisters. It's just that the school choir takes up time that I desperately need for my homework."

Philip nodded to show he understood.

"In a remote way a school is like the world in which you will grow up or like the university to which we hope you will go. In any world you must give as well as take. I admit I don't do much for the community but I do serve on committees and I do take trouble to find out what the council are up to—and I generally lend a hand if I can. So does your mother—she's a real worker for the hospital. Of course we could both use the time for something else but, as I say, I think everybody must give."

"In other words," said Ann, "you think I ought to go on singing in the choir."

"Yes, if that is your only contribution. Later on it probably won't be, you may serve on a school committee or become a prefect, but I don't think you can just opt out of things. At least that's my point of view."

"I'm too junior yet to serve on a committee or be a prefect," said Ann, "but perhaps if I looked around I could

74

find something that didn't take up so much time as the choir. Soon there will be extra practices for the carol service. Quite truthfully, Dad, they can do without me, the standard is pretty high this term."

"Look round then and see what else you can find that is giving service. You couldn't get out of the choir anyway until next term."

Ann gave her father a kiss on the top of his head.

"You are always so sensible. I don't know what I'd do without you."

The school choir was not Ann's only problem. The other was Gemma. Over the years they had got used to sharing a bedroom. Gemma had never learnt to keep her half of the room tidy but Ann accepted this knowing that Gemma had plenty of good qualities to make up. One of her good qualities was that she was usually engrossed in some part she was learning so she didn't talk much, and never nattered on about just anything as Lydia did. But in the last two weeks Gemma had changed and, from Ann's point of view, in the worst possible way.

Gemma was in love with John Cann. It was sad, Ann thought, how idiotic a boy friend could make anybody, even a fairly sensible girl like Gemma. Gemma the silent now had to talk about John, not only while she was dressing and undressing but after they were in bed and Ann was trying to go to sleep. And what boring talk Ann thought it was.

"Of course I've never known a boy before, I mean not like I know John, so I can't make out what he thinks about me. Sometimes he puts an arm across my shoulders, do you think that means anything?"

"I don't know," Ann muttered. "I wasn't there to see him do it."

"I'm not sure he knew he'd done it because he went on talking about Romeo. But, oh Ann, you can't imagine how I felt—honestly it was like an electric shock going through me."

"I hate being pawed," said Ann.

"I wish you could see him, Ann. He really is gorgeous-looking. He's got eyes set deep in his head with marvellous lashes and he's very tall. A sort of Greek god really."

"I don't think the gods looked like that," said Ann.

Gemma sighed ecstatically.

"I can't tell you how thrilling it is working with him—you see it's so wonderful because I'm meant to be in love—and, oh Ann, I am—I am—and so would you be if you saw him."

Ann was not having that.

"I wouldn't. I don't go for boys yet—I think I'm too young."

"You wait until you fall in love and then you'll understand. And remember Juliet was the same age as I am and she was one of the great lovers, everybody knows that."

Mrs. Calvert had, of course, spotted at once that Gemma was falling for John and was not too worried. "She may get a little hurt," she thought, "but it will certainly improve her Juliet."

But if it improved Gemma's Juliet it certainly did not improve her work in Gemma and Sisters. Philip had taken Rosie for two rehearsals on her own, carefully teaching her the songs. Now the time had come for full rehearsals. Not of the solos but of the songs with the three girls and Nigs on his drums.

"Why don't you start with 'O dear, what can the matter be?" Then 'The Little Woman'. Then 'Aiken Drum' and finish with 'The Four Presents'?" Philip suggested. "The last is the most difficult for Rosie."

They set off in fine style with "O dear, what can the

matter be?" but after that each song was a shambles. At first they supposed it was Rosie who was wrong but Rosie, almost in tears, defended herself.

"As Gemma and I are singing the same part of course I listen to her, but I knew we should be singing 'Fol rol diddle diddle dol' not 'Perrie Merrie Dixie and Domine' in 'The Little Woman'."

"All right," said Philip, "start again and for goodness sake attend, all of you."

That time Gemma didn't even get the "O dear, what can the matter be?" words right for "Johnnie's so long at the fair" put her into a kind of trance so she stopped singing altogether.

Philip only just kept his temper.

"Here are all the words written out," he said to Gemma. "I did them for Rosie but it seems to be you who need them."

Starry-eyed Gemma looked at him.

"Sorry. I will try."

And Gemma did try but even though she was reading the words she still made mistakes in spite of Rosie's valiant efforts to keep her to the right words.

After Rosie had gone home and Gemma had wandered upstairs to study Juliet and dream about John Philip said to Robin:

"Don't worry, old man. I'm sure Gemma will be all right next time."

"But what's the matter with her?" Nigs asked. "She never forgets words."

Lydia, who had listened to the rehearsal, looked at him scornfully.

"What's the matter with her? I should have thought even a blind person could see that. She's in love."

Lydia could not have startled her parents more.

"In love!" gasped Alice. "At her age!"

"Who with?" Philip asked.

"You are being a bit of a square, Mum," said Ann. "Lots of girls of our age fall in love."

Robin was disgusted.

"Silly idiots!"

"But who with?" Philip asked again.

Lydia gave Ann a despairing glance as if to say "Where have our parents come from?"

"Her Romeo of course. The simply marvellous John Cann."

CHAPTER SIXTEEN

PLANS

LYDIA went to tea with Rosie Glesse. The reason for the invitation was that Lydia would teach Rosie the tap dance.

"I expect it would be kind to ask her here," Mrs. Glesse said. "There is so much more room. I always think those houses look very poky in Trelawny Drive."

"It's not a bit poky inside. There's room for Robin at the piano and me, Gemma and Ann singing and Nigs' drums and Mr. and Mrs. Robinson and Lydie listening."

Marion Glesse had a whiny voice. She began to acquire it when, before her marriage, she became buyer to a large store and felt it became her position to tone down her northern accent. Whining was the only way she knew of which might do this. She whined now because Lydia's accepted supremacy as a dancer was an abiding grievance. She had not been told the real reason why Rosie was replacing Lydia, merely that Lydia could not dance while Miss Arrowhead was away.

"As you know, I am very glad you are dancing in Lydia's place, and whatever you may think I believe you are the better dancer and others agree with me. But I must say I think it's affectation for Lydia to say she can't dance while Miss Arrowhead is away. Look at you taught entirely by Polly."

"Yes, look at me," thought Rosie. Out loud she said:

"You know that doll dance I did in Gemma and Sisters before—well, we've learnt a new version now on our pointes."

"I know, dear, and tell Polly money is no object, you can have as many private classes as she thinks you will need."

Rosie was a tactful child so she did not say what she was sure was true—that with Miss Arrowhead away it was most unlikely Polly could take private lessons.

Rosie and Lydia practised in what Mrs. Glesse called Rosie's Snug. It was a good-sized room with a carpet which rolled up, so it was convenient for dance practice.

"My goodness!" said Lydia throwing herself into an armchair. "I've eaten so much I can't think how I'll dance. Do you have teas like that every day or was it special for me?"

Rosie had not noticed what there was for tea.

"Mum always makes lots of tea. Before they came to Headstone they lived up north and I think she learnt to make all those cakes and baps and things there."

Lydia looked enviously round the room.

"Aren't you lucky! Look at that lovely practice barre and that long glass. I wish I'd got a room like this."

"I'd swop it any day to be part of a family like you. Mum and Dad are marvellous—always giving me things, but what I want is a sister or even a cousin like Gemma."

"She's not much good now she's in love. Are you doing the doll dance again?"

79

Rosie had no conception what hopes Lydia had harboured that this year at last she would dance—with Miss Arrowhead's approval—on her pointes. So she answered casually:

"Yes. But now we dance it on our pointes."

Lydia turned quite white.

"On your pointes!" she repeated. "On your pointes!"

"Yes," Rosie agreed cheerfully. "We worked at it all last term. It's easy stuff of course or I couldn't do it, but I think it will go down better than on demi-pointe like last time."

"Have you told Polly you are doing it?"

"Yes. Mum said she would but I couldn't trust her. Polly didn't care. I didn't tell her it was Gemma and Sisters, just that I was asked to dance at Christmas. Mum wants me to have private lessons but, as you know, with Miss Arrowhead away Polly won't have time."

Reeling back from the shock of hearing Rosie state calmly that she was dancing on her pointes Lydia remembered her half-formed idea.

"You know I said I might help you?"

Rosie nodded.

"I remember."

"Do you suppose you could have private lessons with me, not saying it was me?"

Rosie was enchanted.

"Oh Lydia, what a simply glorious idea! I'll have to think how I explain about the money but I'm sure I'll find a way."

Lydia was feeling better.

"Good. I'm going to try and earn some money. You see I might need it when Monsieur de Clara sends for me." She got out of the chair. "Come on, let's change our shoes and get on with this tap and do remember to smile, last time you danced for me you and Gemma looked as if you were being punished."

Quite unexpectedly the chance to find some other form of service than singing in the choir came to Ann. The school worked hard for school charities. They had a school mission, they had bought dogs for blind people, they had a huge bazaar every year for a charity which helped the old, they sent a lot of needy children away for holidays and they helped spastics. Now and again the school was asked to help a new charity. This happened that term. A speaker came to talk about music for the mentally handicapped. He was a good speaker so he gave a vivid picture of the blank world of those who could never be taught to read or to write, who often did not know how to play and sometimes could not talk. Then he described the coming of music to such children. How even if all they could manage was a triangle it was like letting a ray of light into a dark room. He wanted music brought to all types of mental institutions but he said it would cost money.

"This is a charity I think," he said, "that should appeal to the musical amongst you, so if you are interested I hope some of you musicians will form a committee to see what you can do to help."

The next day one of the senior boys who played in the school orchestra came to Ann.

"If we get this music committee going we are going to want an organizing secretary. You've been suggested. Would you take it on?"

Ann did not need time to think.

"I can't this term because of the choir but I'll resign from that and I could do it next term if that will do?"

At home Ann told her father what had happened.

"Well, that's quick," Philip said, "and I hope it works out all right and gives you more time."

Since he had heard she was in love Philip had kept an eye on Gemma.

"How's Juliet going?"

Gemma's face glowed.

"Marvellously. John Cann is going to be terrific, even Mrs. Calvert says so."

"Do you like him as a person—I mean apart from being your Romeo?"

Gemma blushed.

"Do I!"

"And does he like you?"

Gemma smiled.

"Truly I don't think he ever thinks of me except as Juliet. Oh Uncle Philip, I've never been so happy. Every day is glorious and rehearsal days are too dreamy to be true."

"Good," said Philip. "Long may it continue."

If the children's Gran had been about who loved proverbs she would have said "Man proposes God disposes", for that very next evening there was upsetting news first for Ann and then for Gemma. Ann's message came in the form of a telegram to Philip:

"Please arrange Ann free for recording first week December followed by public appearance."

Gemma's came by transatlantic telephone.

"Darling, I have such wonderful, wonderful news. Imagine your Mummy has had an offer of a T/V series to be made in England. I shall be coming over soon after Christmas. I shall try and get our old London flat so that you can come and live with me again. Won't it be wonderful!"

CHAPTER SEVENTEEN

TROUBLES AHEAD

IT was strange that two intelligent men had misread a contract. But the fact was this had happened to both George Gamesome and to Philip. Like so many contracts and agreements it was not the main part of the contract but a clause printed in small letters which neither of them had noticed. This gave Eli Push and his associates the right to arrange such public appearances for Ann and Robin as might be considered necessary to promote the record.

"I feel to blame for this," George Gamesome told Philip. "I'm much more used to signing these things than you are. I shall make amends by instructing my solicitor to take advice on this contract and see if there is a loophole through which Ann can wriggle out."

But though George Gamesome's solicitor took the highest advice the answer was that the contract was binding. So Ann, furious at leaving her school work and sick with fright at the thought of public appearances, was tied to going to London at the beginning of December.

Robin was disgusted.

"If anybody ought to make a fuss it's me. Now I'd like to make some more records and I'd absolutely adore public appearances, instead they want Ann who turns green when she thinks about it."

Gemma's problem was equally insoluble. If her mother was coming over after Christmas and taking the old flat she would certainly expect her to live there. But how could she? Nobody—not even Mummy—was going to stop her being Juliet and nobody was going to part her from John Cann.

Gemma's first thought had, of course, been John Cann. She saw him now three evenings a week when they rehearsed with Mrs. Calvert. She had heard through the rest of the cast that some of the grand critics from the national papers had come to see his Hamlet and had given him rave notices. If only he knew one of them and somehow they could get him to a rehearsal. Even Mummy would accept the word of a London critic.

"Something awful has happened," Gemma told John before the next rehearsal. "I mean awful in one way though of course nice in others. My mother is coming back from Hollywood after Christmas to make a T/V series. She's taking a flat in London and I am to live with her."

John looked startled.

"Does that mean that you won't be able to play Juliet?"

"If it happens I suppose it does . . ."

John was thinking hard.

"Thank goodness the production is too far ahead to cancel it now. A few weeks back they might have decided on another play."

"But if I can't be Juliet who will?"

John clearly did not consider that was his problem.

"Perhaps they'll engage a professional or they might try Dulcie Culpepper."

Gemma could not believe her ears.

"Don't you care if I play Juliet or not?"

John, in a dim way, felt he was letting Gemma down.

"Of course I do—I think you'll be awfully good, but if you've got to be in London then it will have to be someone else, won't it?"

Gemma lost her temper. She beat the surprised John with her fists.

"You beast! You beast! You only care about Romeo. You're not thinking a bit about me."

Mrs. Calvert came in at that moment. She gave the two an amused look.

"What's the trouble, Gemma?"

Crying by now Gemma poured out her story.

Gemma lost her temper.

"And all he said was they'd get a professional or perhaps Dulcie Culpepper, who is Lady Capulet."

Mrs. Calvert's reaction was much more satisfactory.

"I don't think we need despair yet. I'm sure when your mother realises what good experience this is for you she will allow you to remain in Headstone until after the performance. If that is impossible no doubt you could live in London and come up here for rehearsals. Now dry your eyes and in future don't beat your leading man about. Young actors and young actresses too are proverbially a self-centred lot, as indeed you are yourself, so the sooner you accept the idea the better."

With great skill Rosie had found a means of getting the money to pay Lydia for dancing lessons.

"And I only told the smallest piece of a lie," she told Lydia. "I said as Polly was too busy I was getting one of the seniors to help me. I know you aren't a senior but you do work with the senior class."

"How much money?" Lydia asked.

"I said ten shillings and sixpence a lesson. That's half what Polly charges so it sounded right. I said I had to take the money with me as it wouldn't be easy for the girl to cash a cheque."

Lydia was enraptured. She flung her arms round Rosie.

"Ten shillings and sixpence a lesson! I'll work and work to make you better for that."

Rosie was glad Lydia was pleased but she saw difficulties.

"But where shall we work? Your room is too small and if we work in my house Mum will know at once it's the doll dance and want to know why we're playing it, and I'll have to pretend I'm learning it at dancing school."

With all that money in view Lydia saw no difficulties.

"Doesn't your mother ever go out?"

"Not often when I'm in," Rosie admitted.

Lydia thought and thought then at last she had an idea.

"I know. We'll tell your mother you're teaching me the doll dance—you know, in case you were ill or something. We'll pretend I am your understudy."

Rosie giggled.

"Imagine you understudying me! Still it is a good idea for I can see Mum swallowing that."

On Philip's advice Gemma wrote a very careful letter to her mother. It was, she explained, simply heavenly to hear she was coming home and that she could live with her in London, but she did most awfully want to play Juliet in May.

"You will understand, Mummy, that it's not just that I want to play Juliet but there's a simply gorgeous boy playing Romeo. When he was Hamlet last year some of the famous critics came to see him and they raved about him. As well Andrew Heron is producing. You may not know about him as you have been away so long but any English actor will tell you. Of course I couldn't bear it if I didn't see you so perhaps I could split up my time between here and London or live with you and come here for rehearsals. But please, please, I must play Juliet."

"Well," Philip said when Gemma showed him the letter, "now we must hold our thumbs until your mother answers. I shall pray hard that she sees your point of view."

Gemma threw up her head.

"She'd better for I can promise you one thing—whatever Mummy says or doesn't say I am playing Juliet."

CHAPTER EIGHTEEN

ON THE WAY TO LONDON

IN spite of the upheavals the rehearsals for Gemma and Sisters went steadily on. The first performance was to be on Boxing Day for a giant party for old people's clubs. Philip ignored Gemma being in love, and that she was waiting almost in a state of frenzy for the answer to her letter from her mother, and quietly but firmly expected her to stage manage Gemma and Sisters as usual. One night he said at supper:

"Have you worked out the lay-out, Gemma? Don't forget Rosie has to change into ballet shoes, all those ribbons take time to tie."

Gemma felt shocked at being expected with all she had to think about to bother with the lay-out of Gemma and Sisters. She spoke in a dismissing voice.

"We can do the same as we did at our last concert I suppose."

Philip paid no attention to Gemma's dismissing voice.

"Well what have you decided you will wear? Is Rosie wearing Lydia's frocks or is she to have new ones?"

"Rosie can't wear my dresses," said Lydia, "because I'm much smaller than she is."

"And for another reason," Alice added. "Mrs. Glesse would have a fit if she was asked to put Rosie into Lydia's pink dress. I'm sick of sewing the sequins on. That material hasn't worn well."

"Anyway," said Lydia, "Rosie isn't the sort of girl to wear that shade of pink with sequins."

"I think Lydie's right," Ann agreed. "Our silver dresses are much neater and truly Rosie won't look right in that pink. I never have liked our pinks myself."

"All right," Philip agreed. "Wear the silver this Christmas, may be something new can be managed by Easter. Now, about the lay-out."

Gemma had worked out so many lay-outs she could do them in her sleep but she sounded bored.

"I suppose we'll start with whichever song Robin likes."

"That'll be 'Aiken Drum'," said Robin.

"Then you change places at the piano with Robin, Uncle Philip, while Rosie and I take our top hats off the piano and do our tap dance. That will take us off the stage. Then you sing your solo, Ann—a good long one so that Rosie has time to change her shoes for her dance. Then after Rosie's dance, while I am singing to my banjo, Rosie changes back to her tap shoes, which I've put on the piano for her, and then we will sing our last song with Robin back at the piano."

"Good," said Philip. "Perhaps you'd write that out for everybody. What'll the last song be, Robin?"

" 'The Four presents'."

Ann sighed.

"You would choose that. It's much the most difficult."

"But it's good for Nigs on his drums," Robin reminded her. "And it's no good saying it's difficult for Rosie because actually Rosie is the sort of girl who never makes mistakes."

"All the same," said Philip, "for Rosie's sake we must have a proper dress rehearsal, it's not fair on the child to expect her to hop into Gemma and Sisters unrehearsed."

"Where will you have a dress rehearsal?" Alice asked. "There's no room here."

Philip had that all worked out.

"I thought in the Gamesomes' basement. I'm sure they wouldn't mind."

"I suppose we ought to invite Mrs. Glesse," said Alice.

The family all laughed. They could still remember Mrs. Glesse at performances and, better still, Lydia's imitating her wearing a tea cosy. For Mrs. Glesse, swelling with maternal pride, knew Rosie's dance by heart and followed it with her head first on one side then on the other.

"If Mrs. Glesse has to come there won't be room for anyone else," said Alice. "The Gamesomes' basement is not all that big."

Lydia, busy teaching Rosie her tap dance and coaching her for her doll dance while hoarding away the ten and sixpences, had pushed to the back of her mind what it was going to be like this Christmas when Rosie was taking her place. Now her mother's casual mention of the fact that there would be no room for them at the dress rehearsal brought the knowledge to the front of her mind. She felt a lump the size of a stone rise in her throat. But one thing she knew: however much she minded her punishment she was not going to let the family see. The children were never allowed to get up from the table until the meal was finished so Lydia could not leave the room. Instead, by swallowing and swallowing, she got rid of the lump and, though tears pricked the back of her eyes, not one rolled down her cheeks.

Ann and Audrey Stratford, though both were busy, usually managed to exchange a weekly letter. So Ann had of course written to tell Audrey the awful news about making public appearances. Now Audrey wrote with a suggestion.

"Mum says why don't you come and stay with us and she'll take you to the recording place and to wherever you are making a public appearance. I can't go with you, worse luck, for Dad is being just horrible just now. He won't let me go to school in Switzerland until I've got my 'O' levels. It's absolute nonsense because I'm sure I could take them there and I'll have a much greater chance as a ski instructor if I go and live out there now instead of waiting until I'm old and grey."

Alice was delighted to hear of the offer, for the very last thing she wanted was an expensive two or three days in London just before Christmas. So she told Ann to accept. Two days later she was more than thankful she had when Barry Thomas telephoned.

"I say, Mrs. Robinson, I've got exciting news for Ann. Eli Push has got her a spot on Teenage Trend."

Alice had never heard of the programme.

"What's that?"

"Just the most popular show on commercial T/V. It's live with masses of kids there. There's a recording machine to show which numbers they like most."

"Oh dear!" said Alice. "I'm afraid Ann will hate doing it. What is she to wear?"

"Keep it plain. She's too young for a lot of buttons and bows."

Alice thought he was very silly.

"Can you see Ann in buttons and bows? A friend of ours, a Mrs. Stratford, is looking after Ann, thank goodness, for I'd be no good at a Teenage Trend. My husband is sending you the Stratfords' address and telephone number. Be kind to Ann. She's a shy girl and will hate appearing in public."

"Now don't you fuss, Mrs. R.," Barry said. "We'll treat her with kid gloves."

Alice caught Gemma when she came in that evening. Gemma was very vague for she had just left John Cann and they had been working together at the balcony scene.

"Now will you try and give me your attention, Gemma," Alice pleaded.

Gemma smiled vaguely.

91

"Of course."

"No, your whole attention. I want your help."

Gemma came slowly back to the present.

"What way?"

Alice told her what Barry Thomas had said.

"Ann's got nothing suitable to wear. Will you lend her a dress and choose it?"

Clothes could always hold Gemma's attention.

"You leave her to me. I'll make her try on some of my frocks before she goes to bed. She'll hate it but I'll make her, I promise."

Alice kissed her.

"Thank you, darling. Oh dear, we shall miss you when you go to live with your mother."

CHAPTER NINETEEN

TEENAGE TREND

THAT night before they went to sleep Gemma found Ann a frock which was perfect for her. It was made of dark blue velvet with a small plain collar held in place with a soft bow. Even Ann liked herself in it.

"Of course the collar is much smaller but it's rather like those black plastics we had for the first Gemma and Sisters. I always liked them."

Gemma was trying out ways of doing Ann's hair.

"I like it best on top of your head like you wear it for Gemma and Sisters, but I should think for this it had better hang loose. The kids on Teenage Trend will probably fall for you if you look very young."

Ann was disgusted.

"It's not me they are voting for, it's the song and how I sing it."

"You can think that if you like but it'll be a lot how you look as well. What's the song like?"

Ann hesitated.

"Really it's pretty awful. Hugo Forrest is nearly sick when I sing it and Dad loathes helping me with it. You must have heard me practising it."

"I haven't," Gemma admitted. "You see, when I get back from rehearsal I come straight up here and think over the scene John and I have just done, almost I can hear his voice."

Ann was sick and tired of hearing about John so she hurriedly changed the subject.

"I don't hate the song nearly as much as Mr. Forrest and Dad do. Of course it's Pop but I think it's good Pop. It's about us really. It's called 'Rose-coloured World'. Each verse is about seeing the world through rose-coloured glasses, but the refrain is sad for it keeps repeating 'We are so young—We are so young'."

Because she was staying with Audrey and secretly did not dislike the song she had to record too much, Ann went off to London in fairly good spirits.

"After all," she said to Philip, who drove her to the station, "it's only one week away from school and then I've finished. I know some time, if they want it, I've got to make one more record but I don't suppose that will be until next year."

Philip kept his eyes on the road so Ann could not see his expression. "Poor scrap," he thought, "has it never crossed her mind that she might be a success, which could mean that she will not find it easy to pull herself free?" Out loud he said:

"I blame myself for letting you in for this nonsense, but when it first cropped up it seemed all they wanted was Robin's swirling."

"You couldn't know," said Ann. "Anyway I daresay

Mr. Push is wrong and they won't like me at all. I mean I bet he goes mad over someone fifty times a year and nobody ever hears of them."

Philip nodded.

"One thing I've quite decided on. I don't sign another contract on your behalf without getting you an agent. And it won't be Barry Thomas, much as I like him, it will be a cautious type who reads all the small type."

Ann quite enjoyed recording "Rose-coloured World". For that record she had a backing from a small, well-trained group of singers. The singers were young and pleasant and looked upon Ann's record as all in the day's work. As well they were sincerely enthusiastic about "Rose-coloured World"—so much so that recording with them was a real pleasure. The pianist, a shy young man, was equally enthusiastic in his way.

"It's not my sort of thing," he told Ann, "but if I betted I would take a bet you've got a winner here. All the orchestra think so."

"I don't really want a winner," Ann confided to him. "I mean, my singing this is really a mistake. We thought it was a family thing they wanted."

The pianist seemed to accept that.

"Which only shows that we have less say in what happens to us than we think. But you weren't very likely to keep that voice locked up at home, were you?"

Outside Mrs. Stratford was getting on splendidly with both Eli Push and Barry Thomas. They both liked jolly, breezy women and they were delighted to find her crazy over "Rose-coloured World".

"Well, I'm glad you're in charge of Ann, dear," Eli Push told her. "You know I'm sure they're very nice people but I couldn't feel, when she made her first record, her Dad and Mum appreciated what a chance I was giving the child."

"Oh well," said Mrs. Stratford, "they soon will. I'm sure this will be a hit."

Barry Thomas talked to her about Teenage Trend.

"I'll go with you to the studio of course. We have to be there in the morning for rehearsal, there's a run-through in the afternoon, then we do it live at eight o'clock. You tell Ann not to be upset by anything, it's all a bit hectic and the D.J. who compères the show can be short at times. Well, you can't blame him, compèring a show live when you've a couple of hundred teenagers to hold in check isn't all that funny."

Mrs. Stratford had been trying to remember what a D.J. was—now it came to her.

"Does the disc jockey have to be in the studio all day too?"

"No. In the morning you rehearse with the singers and the orchestra. Then with the producer. He decides how to produce the artists. You know, whether they will want special effects or what-have-you. The afternoon early run-through is for the camera crew. The D.J. has his rehearsal without cameras around six o'clock. When that's over you can take Ann to get something to eat in the canteen and then she can rest until it's time for her to dress and make-up. They'll tell her about that."

There were five days before the Teenage Trend show, and for those days Mrs. Stratford gave Ann a lovely time. In the mornings she took her to places of interest, such as St. Paul's Cathedral. This was really a labour of love on Mrs. Stratford's part because places of interest were not what she called "her cup of tea".

What Mrs. Stratford liked was to go window shopping or, better still, actual shopping but, as she told Audrey, "I knew where I was with Ann so it's been an educational week. But my poor feet! I wonder why it is that all places you ought to see are so hard to walk on."

In the afternoon they went to a theatre or a cinema. Not really the sort of plays and films Ann would have chosen but she enjoyed them all. Then, after a huge tea, they would go back to the Stratfords' house, where Audrey was rushing through her homework to have time for Ann in the evening.

It was on their last afternoon that something surprising happened. They had been to see a film starring Julie Andrews. Afterwards they went into a nearby café for tea. It was a gay garish place full of boys and girls drinking coffee, there was a radio blaring out a Pop programme.

Ann was just settling down to eat a slice of most luscious-looking coffee cake when a man's voice on the radio said: "How do you like this? It's the first recording of a voice of which it's my guess we shall hear a lot more. 'Ye Frog and Ye Crow'. The singer is Ann Robinson. Little brother Robin is at the piano."

Ann gazed with startled eyes across the table at Mrs. Stratford, the mouthful of cake she was about to eat still on her fork. It was the strangest sensation. There in this café to hear yourself singing, and singing, her critical ear decided, not badly though she was never at her best with Robin's swirled tunes.

As Ann's voice swung round the café everybody seemed to quieten down—or was she imagining that? Surely all these strangers weren't listening? Without moving Ann sat silent until the last line when, with a snap, the poor frog was swallowed. Then she knew people had listened for there was a burble of laughter.

Mrs. Stratford did not know Ann had just heard herself for the first time.

"Of course that tune's not a patch on 'Rose-coloured World'," she said, "but you sang it ever so well. Imagine hearing yourself talked about like that! Isn't it thrilling?"

Ann ate some cake to calm herself down.

"I suppose it is though really I didn't feel it was me. I wish Robin had been here, he'd have loved it."

The Teenage Trend programme was, when Ann tried to look back on it, a blur. All day people seemed to talk round her as if she wasn't there.

"We'll have her just singing straight," the man who seemed to be in charge said. "The choir can be just off left."

A woman in a white overall came up to Mrs. Stratford.

"She doesn't want any make-up really but bring her to the make-up room at 7.15. Has she eyelashes?"

Mrs. Stratford didn't need to ask Ann for that answer.

"No. Nothing like that."

Then a hairdresser arrived.

"I shan't touch her," he told Mrs. Stratford. "Just a brush out, that's all she wants."

When it came to the actual singing Ann felt more detached than ever.

"She can just stand still when she's finished, George," somebody said. "Then you cut to the D.J."

George was evidently the chief camera man.

"O.K.," he agreed.

"Alf," someone called out, "you noted that. You take her away as soon as George has moved off her."

Alf, a spry little man who seemed to move as fast as a grasshopper, shouted:

"O.K., boss. I've got that."

This went on all day. Nobody ever spoke directly to Ann, treating her, she thought, as if she was a tiny child or perhaps a mentally backward adult. But everyone was very kind and, after she had sung at the first rehearsal, almost respectful.

The actual performance, which she had dreaded all day, was very easy. The hoard of teenagers who were the jury took their job seriously, keeping quiet during an actual performance. Ann, who was sitting on a chair off the set, was fetched by Alf. Even though he held her arm he didn't speak directly to her.

"We're on next," he told Mrs. Stratford, "and unless I've lost what wits I ever had we're getting the vote."

Alf led Ann to the side of the set and put her to stand against a pillar. Then, before she was expecting it, she was bathed in floodlight and the D.J. was saying: "This is Ann Robinson. Ann is singing 'Rose-coloured World'."

As always when she was singing Ann thought of nothing else. This time too she was not alone for there was the choir off stage, who backed her beautifully. She did not think about it but at the back of her mind she knew she looked nice in Gemma's frock and that helped. She had nothing to do but sing, there was no worry about getting off stage, Alf would see to that. So giving the audience all she had Ann sang.

CHAPTER TWENTY

THE SURPRISINGNESS OF ANN

At home of course the family was glued to the television set. It was quite an occasion for Pop programmes were discouraged by Philip, so unless he was out they were seldom heard. From Philip's point of view Teenage Trend was a particularly trying programme. It seemed to be made up of one shaggy group of young men after the other singing and playing indifferently. He knew Robin and Lydia thought him hopelessly square, so he did his best in an interval for commercials to find something nice to say.

"There is one good point. The jury seem to know their own minds—rather a good lot. They won't be dragooned into giving marks they don't think the performance deserves."

"Oh, I do hope they give lots to Ann," said Gemma. Alice smiled.

"Don't hope too hard for, you know, I don't think Ann will thank you."

"Too right," Philip agreed. "What Ann hopes for is to sing this once and then oblivion."

"It makes me feel sick," said Lydia. "Imagine if it was me waiting to dance! I'd be praying so hard I'd get all the marks there were I wouldn't be able to think of anything else."

"Don't talk about it," Robin agreed. "Oh, my goodness, if only I had Ann's chance!"

The system on which the show ran was that each member of the audience had a button to press. When the judging took place huge score boards appeared on the screen and a needle showed how many marks each group or individual contestant was awarded. The jury watched the needle and took their fingers off the button when, in their judgment, the needle had reached enough marks. As fingers ceased pressing the needle grew thinner and thinner until it faded away but, as it faded, a star appeared to register the final marks.

"Nobody has got even a hundred yet," said Gemma, "and those boards could go to 250, imagine if . . ."

The D.J. was back. He had remarkable ability in making the outside audience feel just as important as those who were there.

"You are now going to hear somebody new. Ann Robinson. Ann has made two records. The first was 'Ye Frog and Ye Crow' but what she is going to sing now is her latest song only recorded this week. 'Rose-coloured World'."

Gemma studied Ann from a viewer's angle. That frock she had chosen was dead right for her, it made her look even younger than she was but it was well cut and sophisticated. The screen did nothing for Ann's looks. She had rather pronounced features and, if anything, they were more pronounced on the screen than off. "But," thought Gemma, "in a sort of way it's much better than prettiness, she looks a person."

"Bless her, bless her!" Alice thought. "Even in this silly song she means every word." Then she thought again. "But is it so silly?" for as Ann's voice died away on the first refrain "We are so young. We are so young" she found her eyes full of tears.

Lydia and Robin had their minds fixed on marks. They were watching like lynxes each time the camera left Ann for a second to focus on the jury, and what they thought they saw enraptured them. First Robin dug a proud elbow into Lydia and soon Lydia returned it by nudging Robin so hard he nearly fell off his chair.

"We are so young. We are so young." It was the last refrain. For a moment the camera lingered on Ann's face then they were back with the D.J. He silenced what sounded almost hysterical applause.

"Thank you, Ann. That was wonderful. Now, jury, fingers on your buttons please. How many marks for Ann Robinson singing 'Rose-coloured World'?"

It was like an auction sale. Lydia and Robin, far too excited to sit still, bounced about shouting the figures.

"Sixty. Eighty. A hundred and ten. Nobody has got as high as that. A hundred and eighty. Look! Look! Look! She's over the two hundred!"

At the studio Ann seemed the only calm person. She found Barry Thomas almost kissing Mrs. Stratford.

"She's made it! She's made it! In five weeks she'll be in the charts. Two more weeks and she'll be at the top."

"What happens next?" Mrs. Stratford asked, mopping her eyes for she was crying with excitement.

Barry Thomas was just starting to tell her when Ann joined them.

"What happens next is we go home." She looked at Barry Thomas. "We haven't got to do any more, have we?"

"You've got to wait for the final result though it's a certainty," Barry said. "The kids ate you. But you all have to go on to hear the result."

It was like an auction sale.

As Barry had said the final result was a foregone conclusion. Ann had romped home. As before Alf had placed Ann on to the side of the stage and the D.J. came over and fetched her.

"So you chose Ann," he told the jury, "and I don't blame you. Quite a voice this little girl has."

All the way home in the car Mrs. Stratford wanted to go over the glories of the evening but Ann prevented her.

"It's over, thank goodness," she said. "I do hope Audrey is still up."

"Of course she will be," said Mrs. Stratford. "She'll be much too excited to sleep. I expect she'll have supper with us."

Audrey was up and did have supper with them but she was not excited.

"Sorry I didn't hear you," she told Ann. "I did mean to switch you on but I forgot."

"Really, Audrey!" said Mrs. Stratford. "Not to listen to your best friend!"

But Audrey and Ann only laughed, they understood each other.

No one expected Ann to come home like a conquering hero and of course she didn't, but went back to school as if nothing had happened. Naturally almost all the school had listened to her and a good deal of back slapping went on, but it soon died down for lack of response from Ann.

"All the same," Philip told Alice, "we haven't heard the last of this."

They had not. The next move was a visit from Barry Thomas. Philip met him at the music school.

Barry Thomas was not one to beat about the bush.

"I want you to let me be Ann's agent," he said.

Philip tried to explain.

"Ann doesn't want to go on with this. Both I and her singing teacher want her to try for a musical scholarship but she won't. She's set her heart on Oxford."

Barry Thomas nodded.

"I know. You had an eye on opera. Well, she'd hate that. Dressing up and make-up and all the rest apart from having to act. But in my care she would make recordings and a few—a very few—public appearances. This way she could make a lot of money without upsetting too much her normal routine."

"I don't think she wants to do it at all. I know she must do one more recording with perhaps another public appearance but that's all."

"Can I talk to Ann?" Barry asked.

"Of course," Philip agreed. "But you're wasting your time. I know how she feels."

Philip was wrong. Barry came round that evening and talked alone to Ann. What he said or promised her family had no idea, but after half an hour Ann called her father in.

"Dad, I want Barry to be my agent."

Philip was amazed.

"What! But, darling, are you sure?"

Barry nodded.

"She's sure. And you'll find it a very special contract and Ann knows I shall stick to it."

"I know," Ann agreed, "so will you sign it, Dad?"

CHAPTER TWENTY-ONE

ROAST CHESTNUTS

As always happens Christmas sneaked up as if it was wearing felt slippers. It seemed as if one day the papers were saying forty-five shopping days until Christmas, then the next day Christmas was two days away.

Gemma was not looking forward to Christmas for there would be no rehearsals for John Cann was going to his home in Newcastle. Worse still, there had been no answer at all to her letter to her mother—at least no answer to what she had asked. Her mother wrote her usual weekly letters full of chat and her excitement at coming home to England and her joy that she would be seeing Gemma, but she never mentioned "Romeo and Juliet".

"I wonder if your letter could have gone astray," Philip suggested.

But Gemma understood her mother.

"No, this is a thing she does, usually when she doesn't like something. She makes it seem it never happened by not talking about it."

"But she said she was coming soon after Christmas. If she is plans have got to be made, and certainly the university must be told now if you can't play Juliet."

Up went Gemma's head.

"No need to worry about that. I'm playing Juliet. And I'll tell you another thing. You know in that letter I sent Mummy I told her Andrew Heron is producing. And I said she mightn't know about him as she's been away but any English actor would. Well, Mummy wouldn't like that and I should think she's finding out."

"You know your mother and I don't," Philip agreed. "but I do hope she answers soon for, in spite of all you say, I shall feel happier when it's settled."

Every year Gemma's mother sent a huge box of Christmas presents all beautifully gift wrapped. This year the box arrived on Christmas Eve. Undoing the outside packing of Gemma's mother's box and placing the individual parcels under the tree had become part of Christmas.

The contents of all the parcels were expensive but were not always a success, for she seemed sometimes to forget what the Robinsons were like. This year amongst the presents there was an envelope for Gemma marked "Not to be opened until Christmas Day".

Robin was squeezing his own parcel trying to guess what was in it, but he was looking at Gemma's envelope.

"I bet it's money," he said. "I wish people would send me money. I'd soon have a honky-tonk piano if they did."

Ann was feeling her parcel.

"Mine's a book."

Gemma grinned at her.

"Don't fuss. I told Mummy about a book you wanted."

Lydia's was a small parcel.

"Mine certainly isn't a tutu this year. Imagine, I've never worn that simply gorgeous tutu she gave me. It makes me sick."

Robin was shaking Philip's parcel.

"I believe Dad's got cuff links again. He'll have to wear them this year if he sees your mother, Gemma. Do you remember the ones last year made like violins?"

Every year Philip and Alice decorated the tree after the children had gone to bed. They left it lit up so that it was seen in all its glory when the children came down on Christmas Day. It was a happy, peaceful time that both Alice and Philip had grown to love.

"I feel," Philip had once said, "that as we decorate the tree the spirit of Christmas creeps through the house."

That year Philip was quiet. Presently he said:

"This may be the last year of this sort of Christmas."

Alice looked up startled from the ornament she was fixing to a branch.

"Why?"

"Like it or not Ann is getting quite famous."

"I know," Alice agreed, "but she'll handle that. She'll

be the last of our birds to leave the nest. But I'm afraid we may not have Gemma next year."

"I suppose she and her mother could both stay here," Philip suggested.

Alice laughed.

"You don't know my sister Rowena. Heaven forbid she wanted to come here for Christmas. That would turn Christmas into a nightmare."

Philip fixed the star to the top of the tree.

"We've got used to Gemma, she's family. If she's not here Christmas won't be the same."

Alice sighed.

"I know but I suppose, like it or not, we've changes coming."

First thing in the morning, before she touched her stocking, Gemma opened her mother's letter. At once she jumped out of bed and threw her arms round Ann's neck.

"Oh, Ann, I can stay! I can stay! Mummy says she didn't write before because she was making enquiries. I guessed that was what she was doing but I didn't think she'd tell me. Imagine, she wrote to Charles Rooke!"

"Who is Charles Rooke?"

"You know, the man who produced 'Rebecca of Sunnybrook Farm'. You remember him. Well, he told Mummy being produced by Andrew Heron was a big chance for me, but he said something else—guess what?"

Ann held up a needlecase.

"Isn't this pretty? I can't guess—how could I?"

Gemma was hugging herself with pleasure.

"He said he had heard of John and was already booked to come and see him. Imagine when I tell John that!"

Ann pointed to Gemma's stocking.

"Give us a treat and don't mention John all day. Open that before the others come."

Gemma got no chance to do that for the door flew

open and Lydia and Robin, clutching their stockings, rushed in. Robin bounced on to the end of Ann's bed and Lydia on to Gemma's.

"Are Mum and Dad awake?" Ann asked.

"Must be," said Robin. "We shouted happy Christmas outside their door."

"Anyway," Lydia pointed out, "they have to get up soon for church." She emptied her stocking. "Oh, look, a hair net and a hair ribbon and talc for my dancing lessons."

"I've just remembered," said Ann. "This will be my last stocking. As I'm being confirmed next year I shall be going to early service next Christmas."

Robin had his mouth full of Mars bar.

"I should think you could have your stocking at breakfast."

"It wouldn't be the same thing as a family opening," Ann pointed out. "So I shan't have one. I daresay Mum will put the extras for me under the tree."

"Look, a new purse," said Lydia. "But I can't use it because I'm saving."

Gemma had been trying to tell her news.

"I've heard from Mummy. I can stay here until after 'Romeo and Juliet'."

Robin was playing with a pencil which wrote in four colours.

"We never thought you wouldn't. Nigs bet his father a shilling you'd stay."

Alice in her dressing-gown came in.

"A happy Christmas, darlings. Will you see breakfast is ready by the time we get in, Ann? It's sausages."

It was a glorious Christmas Day—one they always remembered because by next year there would be changes. Ann going to early service and Gemma probably living with her mother.

"I don't like changes," said Lydia, "not at Christmas. I want it to be like it's always been for ever and ever."

Alice smiled.

"Dad and I were saying something like that when we decorated the tree last night, but I'm afraid it can't happen. Children grow up you know."

After Christmas lunch and the present opening the family sat round the fire roasting chestnuts.

"Wouldn't it be exciting if we could see us next year " said Lydia.

"It depends," Philip pointed out. "You mightn't like what you saw."

Lydia gave the chestnut roaster a shake.

"I bet we would. Ann top of the charts."

"Thank you very much," said Ann, "but I don't want that."

"Me top of the charts then," Robin suggested. "I'd love it."

Lydia grinned at Gemma.

"You acting in something with John I suppose."

"And you?" Philip asked.

Lydia sniffed the chestnuts.

"I'm sure they're done." Then she slid her eyes round to look at Philip. "Very nice things are going to happen to me. You wait and see."

CHAPTER TWENTY-TWO

THE FIRST CONCERT

BECAUSE she had coached Rosie in her doll dance and had really improved her performance Lydia had hoped not to mind too dreadfully that she was not taking part in Gemma and Sisters. On Boxing Day she found this was not going to happen.

Always before a concert the same routine went on. Alice would say:

"I want all your costumes, shoes, top hats, the lot on the spare room bed so I can see everything before I pack."

Philip, usually immediately after breakfast for he often worked during school holidays, sorted the music and made Robin sort his. Normally there were protests about this. Robin nearly always had a grumble.

"It wouldn't matter if I didn't take my music. Nigs and I never look at it."

"It's a good rule to take it," Philip would say calmly. "Remember if you fell down some steps or anything silly like that I'd have to play in your place."

Usually Lydia was another grumbler.

"I wish you wouldn't pack my dance music. I might want to practise it. Robin can play just for that."

Philip had always the same answer.

"One of my nightmares is my turning up for a concert without your music. I couldn't face having to tell you that you couldn't dance."

That Boxing Day there was the same rushing about. The usual search for Ann's hair ribbon. The usual sort of tense feeling because it was a concert day, but none of it had anything to do with Lydia. To rub salt into the wound there were several excited calls to and from Rosie —or rather from Rosie's mother.

"Rosie says is she right in thinking she gives her tap shoes to Gemma when she changes for her dance?"

Then Alice rang Mrs. Glesse.

"I always make the girls up a little. I forget if I did that last time Rosie stood in for Lydia. Shall I make her up too or will you do it?"

Then it was Mrs. Glesse again.

"I forgot to ask are the girls arriving dressed or are they dressing at the Town Hall?"

Lydia had made a vow to herself that however bad things were she was not going to let anyone see how much she minded. So, though it was a horrible morning, cold and blowy with a feeling of snow in the air, she sneaked up to her room, put on her outdoor things and went for a walk.

Boxing Day is not a good day for walking in a town. All the shops were of course shut and the dustbins crammed with Christmas remains, which always somehow have a sad look. A few houses whose owners did not know that Christmas decorations must not come down until Twelfth Night had even put the Christmas tree out for the dustmen to take away. Nothing looks more miserable than a done-with Christmas tree with a few tatty bits of tinsel still hanging to the branches.

Try as she would Lydia found everything making her worse, not better. The bitter wind stung her face and made her eyes water. Soon she was crying.

"It's because it's Boxing Day I feel so awful," she told herself. "On other days I'll be doing things and I won't mind so much. But today I'm too miserable to live."

There was the sound of a brake going on suddenly and a car stopped beside her. She peered at it through her tears and saw Mr. Gamesome inside with Nigs and his drums.

"Hullo, Lydie," he said. "Get in. It's a horrible day for walking. We are just taking Nigs' drums to the Town Hall."

Lydia tried to rub the tears off her cheeks with the back of her glove.

"No, thank you, I want to walk. But the wind does make my eyes run."

Nigs guessed what the trouble was.

"Come on," he said opening the door. "There's heaps of room for us both in front."

George Gamesome of course knew about Lydia's punishment but he had forgotten about it, now it came to him. "Poor kiddie," he thought. "It's tough on her." Out loud he said:

"Haven't you got that box of peppermint stuff you were given yesterday, Nigs? Give Lydie a lump of that, nothing like it when you are cold."

"What did you get for Christmas?" Nigs asked. "Look at the back, see my new drum."

It was difficult to go on feeling miserable with your mouth full of peppermint lumps, and neither Mr. Gamesome nor Nigs were the sort of people you could be miserable with for long. At the Town Hall Mr. Gamesome gave Nigs two shillings.

"You'll find a fellow in uniform inside. Give him this and he'll help you with the drums and say where they ought to go."

Mr. Gamesome was quite right—the uniformed man came out and soon he and Nigs had taken the drums inside the Town Hall. Mr. Gamesome said:

"I suppose you aren't interested in skating, are you, Lydie?"

"I can't do it much," said Lydia, "but I like watching it. Why?"

"Well I'm supposed to go to the opening of 'Cinderella on Ice' at the Icedrome tonight. I'm a director of the place. They've sent me a couple of tickets but my wife's backed out, says it gives her chilblains, and of course Nigs is in here with his drums. I suppose you wouldn't care to come, would you?"

Suddenly the black day had turned into a glistening day. It was as if Lydia had found a bleak winter wood full of violets.

"Oh, I'd like to more than you'll ever, ever know. Will you ring Dad and ask if I may? He's in to lunch."

"O.K. I'll drop Nigs in on you this evening and pick you up at the same time. Wear all the warm things you've got."

Gemma and Sisters was an enormous success. The old people simply would not let the children go. They had to do everything twice and Ann sang three different songs. Mrs. Glesse, her head wagging from side to side as Rosie danced, was enraptured.

"It really is a smart little show," she said to Alice afterwards. "I don't wonder they just ate my Rosie, she certainly looked a dream."

Alice could have laughed for whatever else solid, pink-cheeked Rosie looked it was not a dream.

"She was very good indeed. See you tomorrow, Rosie. Come on, children, it's time we were home."

Chattering, laughing and thoroughly over-excited Ann, Robin and Nigs, who was coming to supper, climbed into the car.

"Now listen," Philip said, "I know it will be hard but play the concert down when Lydie gets in. There is no need to tell her how splendidly it went, it will only add to her punishment."

Philip need not have worried. Lydia had loved every minute of her evening and was delighted to brag about it.

"You poor things!" she said as she sat down at the supper table. "While I was having a simply gorgeous time I thought of you poor beasts slaving away in the Town Hall."

CHAPTER TWENTY-THREE

THE HOLIDAYS

THAT was Lydia's only good evening while Rosie was dancing in her place. It was not that Alice and Philip didn't try, they arranged everything they could think of to keep her amused, but nothing else worked. For one thing, at the parties—and she went to a lot of those—there were too many questions.

"Why aren't you in Gemma and Sisters at the Winter Garden tonight?"

"Why is Rosie Glesse dancing instead of you?"

"Why aren't you doing Gemma and Sisters any more?"

Of course Lydia had her answers—grand answers that ought to have shut people up.

"Miss Arrowhead doesn't like me dancing in public unless she has coached me herself."

"If I've time I'll be doing Gemma and Sisters at Easter, only of course Miss Arrowhead will want me for extra lessons by then."

"Well Rosie Glesse stood in for me when I had that bad hip so Dad thought she should be asked to do it again. It's only until Miss Arrowhead is back. She's scared I'll get into bad habits—you've no idea how she fusses about me."

But somehow even to her own ears these excuses didn't ring very true and Lydia was sure none of the children believed her.

Then one day Gemma showed her something in a newspaper. It was pure accident Gemma had seen it and she only showed it to Lydia to cheer her up, for however brave a face she put on things they all knew she was miserable.

"Look. I saw this in Uncle Philip's *Times*."

Lydia took the paper. "Ambitious mothers," the article stated, "should notice that Monsieur de Clara is moving his dancing school and company from the south of France to London. He intends later in the year to rent a theatre and give a full season of his ballets. Monsieur de Clara is probably the best teacher in the world so to

"He is very choosey when it comes to picking girl dancers."

learn from him will be a feather in any dancer's cap. One
word of warning though: he admits he is on the look ou
for talented boys but he is very choosey when it come
to picking girl dancers."

Lydia looked at Gemma, her face turning first white
and then red.

"Oh, Gemma! And remember he said 'One day I wil
send for you for an audition. Then we'll see.' Oh,
wonder when he's coming to London."

Gemma began to wish she had not shown Lydia the cut-
ting, she was capable of doing such silly things.

"Don't forget I told you I would help pay your fare i
you got the chance of an audition, but I'll only do it i
Uncle Philip and Aunt Alice know all about it and make
all the arrangements."

Lydia thought of her savings safely hidden away. She had plenty of money to pay her own fare to London. To Gemma she said:

"You're an angel and I won't forget."

Just before the end of the holidays Barry Thomas came down to talk to Ann about plans. He had brought a song with him. Philip was out so he played it for her.

"It's rather a subtle tune we think. If you like it we'd like to cut the record next month."

Ann leant against the piano.

"Right at the beginning of my school term. We go back next week."

"I've thought of that but I promised you we'd steer clear of your school if we could, so I plan you need only miss one day. If we can start bright and early on the Friday you should, all going well, be home Sunday night."

Ann listened to the music. Like "Rose-coloured World" this certainly had something, a queer haunting quality. It was called "If you were me". When Barry had finished playing she said:

"I don't like it as much as 'Rose-coloured World'."

Barry laughed.

"You can't expect a 'Rose-coloured World' more than two or three times in your lifetime, but it's my bet this will make the charts."

"But not the top," said Ann.

Barry laughed again.

"You can't expect to sit up there for ever and ever. If we hit the charts at all we shall be pleased."

"Do you want me to do one of those public appearances again?" Ann asked.

Barry was pleased with himself.

"I promised you if I was your agent I would see you weren't worried. Well, I've fixed another Teenage Trend for you and guess what? It's on your half-term holiday."

Ann did not believe in wasting time. Briskly she took the music off the piano.

"All right," she said. "That'll be O.K. I'll learn this right away."

Barry looked amused.

"I've not come all this way to Headstone to play 'If you were me' through once. If that were all I would have posted it to you together with your recording schedule. No. I've come to see your father."

"What about?"

"A new contract—you've made three records so we start a new contract and I want to talk about money. You're earning a lot pretty fast, you know."

Ann was surprised.

"Am I?"

"Of course. And we've got to decide what you want to do with it. Most of it will have to be saved for you until you are grown up, but what do you want to do with the rest?"

Ann, who had never had any money, was confused.

"Do I decide or does Dad?"

"You I should think. Your father will explain but you ought to be thinking about it."

The last Gemma and Sisters concert was the day before Gemma's new term started. It was a very important day for her for in the evening Andrew Heron had called his first full rehearsal. Ann had one more day before her school started. All the same there was a lot of uniform pressing for them all to do. They were in the middle of this when the telephone rang. It was Mrs. Glesse.

"Oh, Mr. Robinson " she gasped into the phone. "It's Rosie. She won't be able to dance at the concert tomorrow, she's got the 'flu. Ever so bad she is. Her temperature is 103."

Philip came back from the telephone with a half smile on his face. He looked at Lydia.

"Man proposes but God disposes. It seems Rosie has 'flu so punishment or no punishment we need you in Gemma and Sisters tomorrow night."

The moment tea was over Lydia was on the telephone to Polly.

"Oh, Polly, Rosie has been dancing instead of me in Gemma and Sisters—no it will take too long to tell you now—well, she's been dancing that doll dance you taught her and there's Gemma and Sisters tomorrow. Please could I do the doll dance? You see, Dad knows the music. . . . Oh, thank you, Polly. Yes, I know it, perfectly truthfully I do."

Triumphantly she rushed into the kitchen where Alice and Ann were washing up.

"Guess what? Miss Lydia Robinson is going to dance on her pointes. And she's got permission."

CHAPTER TWENTY-FOUR

THE DEAN STEPS IN

To Lydia there never was a concert to equal that last one of Gemma and Sisters. It was a rather special occasion. It was one of the concerts organised by George Gamesome's Rotarians. There was a dance in aid of a fund for old people and in an interval a cabaret of which Gemma and Sisters was the star turn. It was at the Winter Garden which was, in the children's opinion, not only the smartest place in which they performed but had the added advantage of having a superb lighting system, so that the stage could either be bathed in any colour they liked or on their individual turns they could be picked out in a spotlight. Used as they were to makeshift stages and church halls refinements like coloured lights meant a great deal to them. Then there was Charles Rumage. He was the manager of the Winter Garden and an old friend of them all. He was very pleased to see Lydia.

"Hullo! ! I wasn't expecting you. I was told you weren't dancing this Christmas."

"I wasn't," Lydia told him. "You see my teacher is away so Rosie Glesse has been dancing instead of me but she's got 'flu."

Charles Rumage turned to Ann.

"We're very honoured to have you, my dear. You certainly have hit the jackpot and I'm not surprised."

Ann was not shy with Charles Rumage.

"It's luck really—I mean they found 'Rose-coloured World'."

"The kids are going to scream for 'Rose-coloured World' tonight, will you sing it if they do?"

Ann looked at Philip.

"Will I?"

"Well perhaps this once but don't make a habit of it."

All this time Gemma had been standing quietly in the background—an unusual place for her. Now Charles Rumage noticed her.

"Hullo there! And what have you been up to since 'Rebecca of Sunnybrook Farm'?"

"I'm working at Juliet. I'm going to act her in the university production in May."

To Charles Rumage one amateur show was very like another. He was privately surprised that Gemma was allowed to take part.

"That'll keep you busy," he said lightly and turned his attention to Robin and Nigs.

Gemma was surprised how hurt she felt. For once she wished that she was not in the university production but could have said she was going to do something grand.

Not that she would want to act with anybody else but John. It was just that she hated people like Mr. Rumage not to be admiring.

Because Ann was now a star and Lydia, dancing in public for the first time since last Easter and dancing on her pointes was at her very best, Gemma felt her song fell flat. She had chosen an old favourite "I saw three ships", and technically she sang it as well as usual but somehow she could not get over to her audience. It was as if every part of her—her fingers on the banjo, her voice, her personality—had slowed down.

"Oh, my goodness!" she thought. "I mustn't be like this tomorrow. I must be at my very best for the first rehearsal."

If Gemma knew her performance was below par nobody else seemed to have noticed. The audience screamed and applauded and was very unwilling to let them go.

"Top hole," said George Gamesome. "I was proud of the lot of you. And you were a sight for sore eyes, Lydie."

Charles Rumage came to their dressing-room.

"Wonderful!" he said. "You certainly knocked them cold, Ann, with 'Rose-coloured World' and it's always a joy to see you dance, Lydie." Then he rubbed Robin's hair the wrong way. "I think you are swirling better than ever and that new drum of yours is a knock-out, Nigs."

Gemma pulled on her overcoat.

"Funny," she thought, "it's hot in here but I'm cold. I suppose it's because I know I was bad. Oh, I do pray I'm not bad at rehearsal tomorrow."

But for poor Gemma there was no rehearsal the next day or for many days for she had caught Rosie's influenza.

Everyone was very kind to Gemma. Mrs. Calvert sent her flowers and Alice stayed home from hospital to nurse her. She was put in the spare bedroom so she would not pass on her germs to Ann and would be undisturbed.

"Now all you've got to do, darling, is to drink as much as you can and take the pills the doctor left for you," said Alice, "and don't worry about anything."

But in those thick dark dreams which are a part of influenza Gemma was always worrying. She dreamt of rehearsals and saw a distorted John working with strange Juliets whose faces she couldn't see, except once when, surprisingly, it turned out to be Mrs. Calvert.

"She's not reacting to treatment," the doctor told Alice. "She keeps asking if she can get up but her temperature isn't normal, which it should be by now. Is she worrying about anything?"

"Well," said Alice, "she hasn't said so but she could be worrying about missing rehearsals for 'Romeo and Juliet' at the university. She's to be Juliet." She smiled. "The children say she's in love with her Romeo but I can't believe that at her age."

The doctor laughed.

"I wouldn't put it past any of them. They grow up very young these days." He was repacking his medical bag. "Do you think you could write to the young man and ask him to send Gemma a letter telling her how the rehearsals are going—you never know it might bring her temperature down."

As she did not know John Cann Alice asked Mrs. Calvert to ask him to write. Mrs. Calvert did better, she telephoned the Dean, who promised to see the letter was written and delivered.

The rehearsals from John Cann's point of view were being very unsatisfactory. His idea of a rehearsal was working over and over again at his scenes. But Andrew Heron was trying to see the play as a whole and with his Juliet not at rehearsals he was working on his big crowd scenes. However, on the day on which the Dean went to the theatre to deliver Mrs. Calvert's message to

John, Andrew Heron was working at the banqueting scene, with Dulcie, as was possible in that scene, doubling both as Lady Capulet and as Juliet.

The Dean, unnoticed, sat quietly down at the back of the theatre. He loved Shakespeare's plays with what for him amounted to passion. He frequently re-read them and, at least mentally, understood how each phrase should sound. What he now heard outraged and disgusted him.

Whatever she might in time learn to make of Lady Capulet, as Juliet Dulcie was appalling. She made no attempt to be a shy, ardent little girl, instead she was. . . . The Dean tried to think what she was and came up with the word voluptuous—yes, that was it, and a most unsuitable word to think of in connection with Juliet. Against her poor John Cann battled in vain. How could he say:

"O, then, dear saint, let lips do what hands do;
They pray; grant thou, lest faith turn to despair."

to a Juliet who was looking like a tigress about to eat him?

As silently as he had entered the theatre the Dean crept out. He went to his study, wrote a note and called to his odd-job man to deliver it.

Gemma was trying to force down a little soup which was her supper when the note arrived. It was quite short.

"Dear Gemma,

Please get well quickly. Your Romeo needs you. The young lady masquerading as Juliet must be breaking his spirit.

Yours sincerely,
A. G. Garland. Dean."

121

CHAPTER TWENTY-FIVE

THE FIGHT

WHATEVER the Dean might think of Dulcie as Juliet Dulcie and her innumerable boy friends thought she was marvellous. It is easy in a university to find supporters for almost any cause. The leaders, who rush about stirring up excitement, believe—at least temporarily—in the axe they want to grind, but many of the followers are in for the fun of the thing and the possibility of a fight. It was this sort of group, started by Dulcie's fans, who decided to campaign for a "Keep university plays for university students" movement. The plan was first to approach the Dean with a petition and secondly, if that failed, to have a sit-in in the theatre. Banners were painted of designs and wording which suited the painters and there were several very vocal meetings in students' rooms. But all this only concerned a minute portion of the students, the majority having no idea that anyone was protesting.

Gemma though, as the doctor had hoped, her temperature went down to normal after she had received the Dean's letter was convalescent for several days, so it was a week before she was able to go to a rehearsal. During that week Dulcie, backed by her followers, had taken over the part of Juliet and somebody else was reading Lady Capulet. Who played what at this stage meant very little to Andrew Heron, all he needed was principals to say the lines while he moved his crowds round them. To give the entire cast the feeling for the play as a whole he allowed the scenes which concerned the actors only, to be run through, but he was not ready to produce them yet, that would come scene by scene when his crowds were trained. Of course John Cann and some of the other actors complained to him that they did not know what he wanted, but he calmed them down.

"I don't know myself what I want yet. Quite soon I'll have these crowds fixed and then I'll concentrate on you." To John Cann he added: "I can't work at your scenes until your Juliet is back. It's no good saying anything to that terrible Miss Culpepper."

Mrs. Calvert took Gemma to her rehearsal. When they reached the theatre Andrew Heron had not yet arrived, but the stage manager and his assistants were chalking the stage to show exits and entrances. John Cann saw them come in and came at once to join them. He forgot to ask if Gemma was better but he did say he was glad to see her back.

"I can't work with Dulcie hanging over me and breathing down my neck."

"What scene is Mr. Heron taking today?" Mrs. Calvert asked.

"Act I Scene 5. You know, the banqueting scene. We have worked at it before. It's full of business for the servants but we do our scene though half the time he isn't noticing."

Andrew Heron came striding up the hall. He shouted to his stage manager.

"Get everybody on for Act I Scene 5."

Gemma got up and walked beside John to the stage. As she reached it the Dulcie supporters, seeing her, began to chant.

"Gemma out, Dulcie in.
Gemma out, Dulcie in."

As always when a lot of people start to shout it is hard to catch what they are saying. Andrew Heron took the megaphone he used at rehearsals from his stage manager and shouted through it:

123

"What the hell is that noise? Complete quiet please."

There was silence for a second and then the chanting broke out again.

"What are they saying?" Andrew Heron asked his stage manager.

"I think it's Gemma out, Dulcie in. There's a group want only university students used in university plays."

At that moment Andrew Heron saw Gemma.

"Hullo, my dear. Welcome back. I shan't overwork you today, I'm going to concentrate on the crowd in the banqueting scene—at least I shall when these yobs stop shouting."

But the shouting went on growing in volume. Then someone made a suggestion to Andrew.

"Perhaps you could let Dulcie do the Juliet scene just for today and by the next rehearsal something would be fixed.

Andrew was outraged.

"Give in to a mob like that! Never." Then he looked round the stage at his serving men, maskers, guests and musicians. They were, he noticed with pleasure, a hefty looking lot. He beckoned to them to gather round him.

"I say, chums, do you think you could throw that lot out so we could get on with our work?"

There were none of Dulcie's supporters in that scene so the young men moved as one. With strange shouts and oaths they leapt off the stage and tackled the rebels.

It was a tough and for many a bloody fight but it was successful. Every shouter was finally ejected and the doors locked against them. For a time they continued to chant outside "Gemma out, Dulcie in" and to beat on the doors but at last they drifted away.

"Well done, chums," said Andrew. "Now to work."

Of course the news of the uproar had reached every corner of the university, so soon after the last of the rebels

124

"We don't want outsiders."

125

had moved away the theatre telephone bell rang. It was the Dean. He asked for Andrew.

"I gather your Capulets and Montagues have got strangely out of hand. I have a scheme which I think should settle the matter. Perhaps you would call in for a glass of sherry before you leave."

Gemma had been so startled by the shouting and the fight that followed that she had not really taken in what it was all about. But Dulcie enlightened her. She sidled up to her just as the rehearsal started and said:

"That was about me playing Juliet. We don't want outsiders acting in university productions. You can play her today but tomorrow will be a different story."

After rehearsal in the Dean's study Andrew heard the Dean's plan.

"I gather the trouble-makers are a very small proportion of the students so I am prepared to take a risk. I propose tomorrow to inform the university that any trouble-maker who is caught will be rusticated, but I have heard their complaint and am prepared to pay heed to it. On an appointed day next week all interested, if they behave themselves, may come to the theatre. There they will hear Shakespeare's balcony scene first performed by Dulcie as Juliet and then by Gemma. Afterwards there will be a ballot."

Andrew was appalled.

"But that lot don't know acting when they see it."

The Dean sipped his sherry.

"I wonder. We shall find that out shall we not."

But Andrew was not happy.

"I couldn't produce the play with that dreadful Dulcie."

"My dear young man, have another glass of sherry. You will not have to. I shall see the theatre is full and, as always in these affairs, we shall find the rebel-rousers are a very small proportion of the whole."

CHAPTER TWENTY-SIX

THE BALLOT

LYDIA had news at last. She had watched the post so long she had almost despaired of a letter ever coming. Then one morning there it was lying on the doormat. There was no mistaking who it came from for de Clara Ballet was printed in large letters on the left of the envelope. Inside was not a letter as she had hoped but a printed form. It said that Monsieur de Clara was holding an audition at the Dickens Theatre at 11 a.m. on Monday, February 9th. Please reply if you are unable to come.

Lydia put the letter in her jumper pocket and, trying to look as though nothing out of the ordinary had happened, she brought the rest of the post to the breakfast table. But inside she was feeling fussed. She wished the audition had not been that Monday the week after Miss Arrowhead was back for it would be much more difficult to miss one of her classes than one of Polly's. She wished too there was someone whose advice she could ask. There was Gemma who always tried to help. But Gemma was no good to anybody now; apart from her being in love there was this fuss about doing a scene from "Romeo and Juliet" so the students could choose between her and somebody called Dulcie. There was of course Ann but Ann was certain to say ask Dad and Mum and what did they know about dancing?

Lydia's real trouble, which she hated admitting even to herself, was Miss Arrowhead. Miss Arrowhead had been so very kind to her, teaching her for nothing and sending her to the drama school. Of course Miss Arrowhead should be told about the audition. But suppose she said she did not want her to go to the audition? She simply could not risk it. This was her great chance.

Philip had talked to Ann about her money.

"Two-thirds is being banked for you so when you go to the university you'll be downright rich, but there is still plenty for you to do as you like with now."

Ann knew one answer to that.

"I'd like to give some to you and Mum, I mean it's silly if I've got the money you buying my clothes and all that, and I'd like Mum to have lots more to spend on the house and housekeeping and doing things you both like."

Philip saw her point.

"All right if that's what you want but for the rest you'll have to think it out. It's your money and you must have the spending of it. I'm sure there are lots of things you want."

But there were not a lot of things Ann wanted. She had simple tastes and would have been embarrassed by the sort of clothes and bits and pieces other girls hankered after.

"I'll keep most of it I should think," she decided. "Some day Robin might want an expensive music education, and I could pay for us all to have a gorgeous holiday next summer."

Then one day bicycling home from school she was joined by a boy called Alick who was chairman of the committee to raise funds for the mentally handicapped. He rode along beside her slowly telling her of an experience he had in the Christmas holidays.

"I'd told my Dad about our music for the mentally handicapped committee. Well he knows a doctor chappie who works at the mental hospital and there's a children's wing there."

"Do they have music?" Ann asked.

"It has just been started so Dad got two tickets and Mum took me to a carol service."

"Were they any good?"

Alick made a face.

"Not really. Well they haven't been doing it long but they were helped out by the piano and someone on the fiddle. I'll tell you something though—they were dead keen. I mean even the worst of them and some of them don't look as if they'd any brains at all hit their triangles or tambourines or what-have-you as if it was something they were proud of."

"Is that all they had—triangles and tambourines?" Ann asked.

"Oh no, the brighter ones played recorders and one kid had a drum."

Ann tried to picture the scene.

"No 'cellos or violins or woodwind or anything like that?"

"No, I told you they hadn't been at it long and anyway I don't suppose many of them could learn anything like that. After all, violins and things cost quite a bit."

Ann had such a wonderful idea she nearly fell off her bicycle.

"But I've got money. You know—'Rose-coloured World'. Do you think you could see that doctor your Dad knows and find out what they could use if they had it?"

Alick was delighted.

"Of course I could. As a matter of fact I'll tell you something, the female who has started the music idea told me. She's a toothy old hag who has been doing this music lark in a lot of mental hospitals. Well she said that when children she'd taught moved on to adult mental hospitals the doctors and nurses said they were easier to look after than most patients, and she reckoned that was because they'd made a bit of music."

Ann rode home with her head in the clouds. Suddenly everything was falling into place. She wouldn't mind making records if sensible things happened to the money, almost she wouldn't mind appearing on Teenage Trends. And it wouldn't only be her own hospital she would help but any place where there were mentally handicapped children.

Although there was an attempted sit-in in the university theatre as a protest against the ballot it came to nothing. The Dean might appear a dreamy scholar with his feet seldom on the ground but when the need arose he was very much on the spot. The same evening as the rebels were thrown out of the theatre he called his staff together.

"We cannot of course have this sort of thing going on—it's anarchistic." He knew that some of his younger lecturers might sympathise with the students so he hurried on. "I am perfectly aware than some feel they have a legitimate grievance. which is why the problem is to be settled democratically by a ballot. Meanwhile we must remove temptation from the hot-headed. I have ordered that every window in the theatre is barred and every door locked. At the same time I would be most grateful if you could organise a patrol who would keep an eye on things and warn off any who are seen hanging about."

As a result of these precautions. on the Thursday when the ballot was to be held. a large and mainly well-behaved audience filed into the theatre. Mrs. Calvert was waiting behind the stage with Gemma. She peered through a door which led into the theatre.

"It's all fairly quiet, dear. I am sure you have no need to be nervous."

Gemma shivered.

"How do you know that when I come on they won't keep shouting 'Gemma out, Dulcie in'?"

"I have faith in the Dean." said Mrs. Calvert trying to sound far more confident than she felt. "He will have everything in hand."

130

And the Dean had. Before Dulcie and John played the balcony scene he came on to the stage.

"What you are about to witness is the result of a demand from a small proportion of you. Because in the opinion of those who should know there was no student suitable to play Juliet . . ." a growl rose on this. The Dean held up his hand. "Kindly do not interrupt. I repeat no student suitable to play Juliet, it was decided to borrow a young professional actress from the drama school— Gemma Bow, who is exactly the age Shakespeare gave his Juliet. You are to see the same scene played twice. First by one of our students—Dulcie Culpepper—and secondly by Gemma Bow. Then there will be a ballot to decide which is the better performer."

The Dean then stepped off the stage and sat down in the front row.

Dulcie's appearance was greeted by enormous applause, foot stamping and shouts from her followers. But when the theatre was packed, as it was that evening, the followers were only a very small part of the whole.

To give some idea of what was happening Andrew Heron had arranged to use a high rostrum on wheels tethered to the side of the stage which was part of the theatre's movable scenery. It had a rail round the top over which Juliet could lean to talk to Romeo. Dulcie had tried to help herself to feel like Juliet by putting on a dressing-gown, which presumably was what Juliet would have been wearing. But Dulcie's dressing-gown was orange velvet trimmed with ostrich feathers. She looked, with her long black hair, very striking in it but not in the least like a Juliet.

As usual John Cann was thinking only of his part. If he had to play a scene with Dulcie this was the one he would have chosen for she could not breathe down his neck, and

131

the speeches were long enough for him to get his teeth into the part.

They played the scene from where Romeo first sees Juliet at her bedroom window.

"But, soft! what light through yonder window breaks?" and they finish where Juliet hears the nurse moving. "I hear some noise within; dear love, adieu!——"

It was presumably nobody's fault for exhaustive search afterwards could find nobody who was to blame, but Dulcie, who was the sort of actress who showed emotion by throwing herself about, loosed her rostrum from its moorings with the result that she and her balcony slowly sailed across the stage.

The effect was very funny indeed. At first the audience struggled with giggles but soon the drifting Dulcie was too much and everybody, even her followers, were howling with laughter.

Dulcie was furious, so furious that she lost her head. She climbed down off the rostrum and stalked down to the front of the stage.

"Beasts!" she shouted. "You beasts!" Then she rushed off the stage.

By the time the rostrum was fixed the audience had calmed down and were waiting to judge Gemma.

On Mrs. Calvert's advice she was wearing a very simple pale blue dress in which she looked very young. But young as she was this was her favourite scene for what Juliet said she was longing to say. All her heart was in her performance and John Cann, feeling this, played right up to her. It was by far the best performance the two had given.

They were rewarded by that greatest of all compliments —a hushed silence, to be followed by thunderous applause.

A ballot was taken but it was a farce, even her own supporters had deserted her. Dulcie scarcely got a vote.

CHAPTER TWENTY-SEVEN

MUMMY

GEMMA'S mother was to arrive in London on the Friday that Ann was recording "If you were me".

"So convenient," Alice said to Gemma. "You and I and Ann can all go to London together."

Gemma looked mulish.

"You know I can't go on a Friday. It's a rehearsal day."

Rehearsals for "Romeo and Juliet" were now almost daily but Andrew Heron did not take most of them. Having fixed the shape of his crowd scenes he usually left them to his second in command, but every week-end he worked with his principals.

Alice knew Gemma too well to argue with her. She took her problem to Philip.

"You don't know Rowena," she told him: "She'll be furious if Gemma isn't there."

"I think Gemma ought to go," said Philip. "It can't matter if she misses one rehearsal, surely somebody must be understudying her."

Alice laughed.

"I'm sure somebody is but it's all kept rather quiet since that students' uproar."

"Go and have a talk with Mrs. Calvert," Philip advised. "She's a sensible type and I think Gemma has a wholesome respect for her."

So Alice took time off from her hospital work and called on Mrs. Calvert.

"Really," Alice explained, "Gemma ought to spend the whole week-end with her mother, but I can see that would be too inconvenient, but I think she ought to be there to meet her on the Friday. She's been very good allowing Gemma to stay with us until after the production for really she wanted her to live with her in London."

Mrs. Calvert's eyes twinkled.

"I'll tell you a secret even Gemma doesn't know. Her understudy is in this school. It was the Dean's idea and really it's very sensible for if Gemma were ill no university student could wear her costume. I've picked a girl who is a good Shakespearean if dull who is just Gemma's size. I am coaching her here and I bring her to watch rehearsals, but except in real emergency she is not to appear as it might cause further trouble."

"Oh dear!" said Alice. "Then Gemma really can't get away on the Friday."

Mrs. Calvert dismissed that regally.

"Nonsense! One Friday won't matter. Andrew Heron must rehearse the scenes that don't concern her. I'll tell him."

So on the Friday in the next week Alice, Ann and a rather sulky Gemma caught the early train to London.

On arrival at the recording studios the same fuss as before was made over Ann, but now she could take everything in her stride.

Gemma and Alice sat in the studio to listen to Ann and, since for the moment nobody was paying any attention to them, Alice decided this was a good moment to talk to Gemma.

"I know you didn't want to miss your rehearsal but don't forget how unpredictable your mother can be. If you greet her with the sort of face you've worn all the morning she'll quite likely change her mind and say Headstone isn't good for you and you are to stay in London."

Gemma was horrified.

"She couldn't! I know she couldn't!"

"Then I know her better than you do," said Alice.

"Why, I can remember when she was about your age she was asked to be a bridesmaid. At first she was very excited and wrote an ecstatic letter accepting, then the design for the dress came. Oh dear, what a scene! She kicked and screamed, in the end for peace we gave in and she wasn't a bridesmaid."

"But that's different. I mean you can't compare acting Juliet with a gorgeous actor like John and being a bridesmaid."

"I'm only showing how easily she can change her mind. If you look cross instead of pleased to see her it could be quite enough."

Gemma could not answer for Ann had started to sing. Alice closed her eyes and gave herself to the music. Even in this rather trite song as Ann's voice rose, backed by a vocal group and the orchestra, it really was a lovely noise. "I wonder," thought Alice humbly, "what I've done to have a daughter with a voice like that."

After the song, before Ann went through it again, Barry Thomas came over to speak to them, but first Gemma had slipped a hand into Alice's.

"Sorry I've been horrid. I am pleased to see Mummy, truly I am, and I'll let her see it."

Sometimes, because she could only talk to her by letter or telephone, Gemma felt out of touch with her mother. But no sooner was she with her than the gap filled and it was as if she had never been away. For one thing good facials and hair-do's defied the years so that in appearance Rowena had changed very little. Her hair was rather a brighter gold and she wore longer and blacker artificial eyelashes. She never had looked like anybody's mother, not in the way Aunt Alice did, and at this meeting she looked less like a mother than ever for she was very slim and the short skirts made her look girlish. But of course she was Mummy and when Gemma saw her walking towards her in the Savoy Hotel she ran to meet her and threw her arms round her.

Rowena kissed her then stood her away from her.

"Let me look at you." Then she smiled. "You haven't grown much, that fur coat still fits you." Evidently she liked what she saw for she patted Gemma's cheek and drew her to her as she greeted Alice.

"How are you, Alice dear, and this must be Ann?" Rowena knew all about Ann for "Rose-coloured World" had reached the American charts. "Poor child!" she thought. "What a drab little thing," but this thought did not show on her face. "Many congratulations on your success, dear."

Rowena ordered drinks, soft drinks for the girls and something stronger for herself and Alice, while she poured out her news. The serial she was to be in for T/V was to be filmed largely in the studio and she had a contract for three more. She expected to be in England for at least two years.

"And isn't it splendid, darling," she said to Gemma, "I can get the tenants out of our flat by May so as soon as this play is over you can come home. Won't we have fun!"

Alice looked sad.

"I hope you'll spare her to us sometimes. We shall miss her."

"In the fall. . . ." Rowena laughed. "Listen to me—autumn I should say—you'll be going to a drama school in London, Gemma, but I'm sure you'll find time to visit Headstone and when Ann comes up to make new records she must stay with us—isn't that right, darling?"

Gemma felt her smile growing stiffer and stiffer. It would soon be February, only three months away from May. In a little over three months were the cousins and Headstone going to be reduced to "I'm sure you'll find time to visit Headstone?" Was it really going to be a sort of proper good-bye?

Luckily for Gemma her mother chose that moment to put an arm round her so she did not see her face.

"I just can't wait for May," Rowena said. "Mummy will be lonesome without her baby."

CHAPTER TWENTY-EIGHT

ALICE'S FIND

THE recording of St. Giles' choir had sold well at Christmas. Nigs' dream of Robin being fabulously rich on the proceeds of "O for the wings of a dove" had come to nothing but he had made a little money which was banked for him. Nigs had made a little money too, less than Robin because he was not a solo boy, but still some money and he was allowed to spend his on a new bicycle. The fact that he was going to have a new bicycle anyway and that probably Nigs' father had paid part of what it cost made no difference to Robin. Here was a grave injustice and it ate into his soul.

"It's not right," he told his father. "Here's me wanting and wanting a honky-tonk piano and never getting it and when I do get some money I mayn't spend it, it is just put in the Post Office which is no good to anybody."

Philip was sympathetic.

"I can see it seems a terrible injustice but where would you put a honky-tonk piano?"

That was a poser. Then Robin had an idea.

"When Gemma goes to London with her mother Lydie can share Ann's room and my honky-tonk can go in Lydie's room."

This caused howls from all the family.

"Oh no, darling! Not a honky-tonk up there," Alice pleaded.

"Thank you very much," said Ann. "When Gemma goes I'll have my room to myself."

Lydia glared at Robin.

"If you think, my boy, you are having my room with its practice barre you've got another think coming."

Gemma said nothing.

"It's just as if I'd gone already," she thought. "Ann didn't say she would be glad to have her room to herself but I can see that's how she feels. I don't believe they'll miss me at all when I've gone. I'll just be like a castle on the sand—washed away with never a mark to show where I was."

Robin's complaint, though it fell on stony ground at home, received sympathy from the Gamesomes.

"Poor old Robin!" said George Gamesome when Nigs poured out the story of Robin's ill-usage. "I must say it's tough if he can't use his money as he likes."

Mrs. Gamesome too was sympathetic.

"I'm not sure what a honky-tonk piano is but I'm sure if Robin gets one it could go into the basement. Now we've had it sound-proofed it doesn't matter what strange noises you make down there."

But even with this splendid offer Philip refused to let Robin have any money.

"If, as I expect, you decide on a musical career you'll want every penny you can save. It's very easy to be a starving musician."

So Robin went around with so big a chip on his shoulder everybody noticed it. The truth was it was the first time he had come face to face with what he considered, not only an injustice but an injustice inflicted by of all people his father, who up till then he had trusted implicitly.

"I don't know what's got into you, young Robin," Mr. Reynolds, the choirmaster, grumbled. "You've had a black dog on your shoulder for weeks, is this the aftermath of a swelled head acquired through singing the solos on our carol record?"

That really was adding insult to injury.

"Of course it isn't. You know I didn't care who sang the solos, at least I didn't except for the money."

"Well you've got some of that," said Mr. Reynolds.

"That's what you think," Robin growled. "But Dad's taken it all."

Mr. Reynolds did not believe that.

"You mean he's banked it for you. Very proper."

Robin could have hit Mr. Reynolds.

"It's not proper, it's mean. He knew I wanted to buy a honky-tonk piano."

Mr. Reynolds shuddered.

"I'm glad your family were spared that horror."

Robin could have kicked him. They were all against him. The world was against him.

"You wait and see, sir," he said. "I'll have my honky-tonk in the end, you see if I don't."

Robin was not the only member of the family with a problem. Lydia was suffering from something she had never suffered from before, she couldn't get to sleep at night. She tossed and turned, puzzling what to do. In five days, then in four days, then in three days, Miss Arrowhead would be home. She would walk in one morning and find her waiting to give her a lesson. And after the lesson quite likely she would tell her all about how the girls had danced in South America. Quite likely too she would have brought her a present—something she could wear in a character dance. What was she to do? How could she treat Miss Arrowhead as if nothing was going on when she knew that the very next Monday she was going to sneak up to London for her audition?

Of course the fact that Lydia was worrying about something and, as a result, was not sleeping was not missed by Alice. At first she tried to help with ordinary remedies, bringing Lydia up a glass of hot milk when she was in bed, making opportunities to be alone with her so that she could confide in her if she felt like it. But it was no good for it was impossible for Lydia to tell her mother about Monday.

"I know what I'll do," Alice told Philip. "I've been meaning for ages to put some of those plastic tiles round her wash basin. I'll do it tomorrow—perhaps she's been feeling rather out of things with Ann going to London and Robin's carol record and Rowena here, a little special attention may be all she wants. Thank goodness Miss Arrowhead will soon be back."

The next morning Alice bought some pastel tinted tiles and went up to Lydia's attic. This had been fixed up as a pretty little bedroom for Lydia and nobody could have failed to guess it was her room. A pair of ballet shoes was tied to the practice barre. There was the woollen leotard she used in cold weather hanging on the door and half out of one of her drawers was the leg of a pair of pink tights.

"Bless the child!" thought Alice, opening the drawer to put away the tights. "Will she ever learn to be tidy!"

Alice took out the tights, folded them and decided to tidy the drawer. It was full mostly of Lydia's dancing things. Tights, socks, briefs and a tunic she had outgrown. Then at the bottom Alice came across a box. She opened it expecting to find other dancing objects such as castanets, instead she found money. Seven ten shilling notes and underneath them a folded piece of paper. She was not meaning to pry, she was just puzzled. Then her eyes widened as she read what was written:

140

"Monsieur de Clara is holding an audition at the Dickens Theatre at 11 a.m. on Monday, February 9th. Please reply if you are unable to attend."

Alice did not fix the tiles round Lydia's basin. She put the box and its contents back where she had found it and went downstairs to have a cup of tea and to think. First of all where had Lydia got all that money? It could of course have been given to her by Gemma but after the last fright when Lydia was lost Gemma was very unlikely to give Lydia money unless she knew how it was being spent. Then where? Surely Lydia must have come by it honestly, she had never been a dishonest child. Yet when it came to her dancing she would consider almost any means fair to further her ends. And this audition was an end she would think supremely worthwhile. Oh, thank goodness Fate had led her to that box, it made her shudder to think of Lydia going on her own to London, but that must be what she was planning.

That night when Alice came back from the hospital she went straight up to Lydia's room where she knew she should be doing her homework. Lydia was certainly surrounded by books but she did not appear to be working. Alice sat down on the bed.

"Lydie, by mistake I found a cardboard box belonging to you in that drawer. There was money and a letter about an audition in it. Were you planning to go to London on Monday?"

For a moment it looked as if Lydia was going to brazen things out. Then she got up and flung herself on her mother.

"Oh, thank goodness you know!" she sobbed. "I hated telling nobody but I was afraid to in case you stopped me. But you won't, will you?"

CHAPTER TWENTY-NINE

MISS ARROWHEAD COMES HOME

ALICE managed to drag out of Lydia the whole story. How, when she had met Monsieur de Clara, he had said "One day I will send for you for an audition."

"Well I knew when he sent nobody would let me go and I had to. Gemma would have given me money for my railway ticket but only if you and Dad knew I was going. Well I knew that was no good so I had to think how to earn it."

Alice stifled a sigh of relief.

"How did you earn it?"

"Rosie. When her mother knew she was going to be in Gemma and Sisters she said she was to have private lessons. Well, I knew with Miss Arrowhead away Polly was too busy to give private lessons, so I thought why not me?"

"So you taught her!" said Alice. "I thought she had improved."

"Polly charges one guinea a lesson so Rosie and I thought ten shillings and sixpence would be fair. I kept all the ten shilling notes but I spent the sixpences. The worst thing was where to teach but in the end we pretended she was teaching me the doll dance in case she was ever ill, so I was able to learn in Rosie's sitting-room."

"What was your plan about Monday?"

"Oh, it was easy. Instead of going to dancing class I was catching the early train. I was telephoning from the station to say I couldn't come to my dancing class because I had toothache and then the same message to school. As the audition was at eleven I knew I could get back just about the time I would have come back from school. I meant to catch Gemma so she wouldn't say I hadn't been there."

"You certainly had it all planned," said Alice.

Lydia nodded.

"I had to. This is the big chance of my life, you do see that, don't you?"

Alice picked up one of Lydia's hands and stroked it.

"I see a lot of other things. Suppose—just suppose— you auditioned for Monsieur de Clara and he accepted you how would you live in London?"

"I suppose in some sort of school. I mean I can't be the only one who has to do lessons."

"And who would pay?"

Pay! Lydia had not thought of that.

"Perhaps I could get a scholarship like I have with Miss Arrowhead."

Alice stuck to her point.

"But if you didn't get a scholarship where did you think the money was coming from?"

Lydia had to face the truth.

"I never thought about money except the £3 10s. I had for London, which is more than it will cost."

"Well, think now," Alice pressed. "You know we aren't rich. Dad doesn't earn all that much with his teaching, we get by but there isn't even money for holidays let alone keeping one daughter in London."

Lydia slowly faced the facts.

"You mean even if Monsieur de Clara said he'd teach me I couldn't learn with him?"

"That's right. Dad and I couldn't find the money. So I'm afraid you must write and explain why you can't come."

Lydia shook her head.

"No. I've got to know. Not just what Miss Arrowhead

143

says but what Monsieur de Clara says. I've got enough money for the fares, will you take me, Mum?"

"You want to go to this audition even though you know it's hopeless?"

"Yes, and I'll tell Miss Arrowhead I'm going. I'll hate doing it but if you'll take me I'll tell her."

Alice gave Lydia a kiss.

"Very well, you shall go. It was very wrong of you to have planned to go on your own, but as I found out in time and you earned the money honestly you shall have your audition. But on one condition. You are not to tell anybody except Miss Arrowhead that you are going. I don't want a word of this to reach your father. He hates not being able to do things for you children, so I'm not going to have him worrying himself sick wondering how to pay for you to have classes in London."

It seemed to Lydia the most monstrous thing to be asked to keep something as important as an audition with Monsieur de Clara secret. Now that her mother knew she wanted to rush round the house telling everybody.

"Tell absolutely nobody?"

"Yes," said Alice firmly. "Absolutely nobody except Miss Arrowhead or we don't go."

Fortunately for Lydia at supper that night all the family were too busy with their own affairs to notice anybody else or they must have noticed that Lydia was bursting with a suppressed secret.

Gemma had just had a private rehearsal taken by Mrs. Calvert with John which had left her deaf and blind.

Ann had come from a Music for the Handicapped meeting where she had been told by the chairman to outline the help she believed she could give. The news of the money she could spend had presented an entirely new picture to the committee and it was decided they could now look beyond Headstone. An idea was mooted for visits to be paid to a selection of hospitals and homes for mentally handicapped children during the Easter holidays. Ann was glowing inside, this was the best of both worlds—a school thing made possible by money earned by her records.

Robin was still brooding on the honky-tonk piano he couldn't have. It is doubtful if all the girls had stood on their heads whether he would have noticed.

To say she would tell Miss Arrowhead about her audition was one thing, to tell her Lydia found out was quite another. The day after her return Lydia turned up for class to find her waiting for her. Miss Arrowhead opened her arms.

"Hullo, darling! I'm back at last and I hear from Polly you've been wonderfully good and patient. But we'll make up for wasted time. I'm going to try and squeeze in some extra lessons for you."

Lydia licked her lips.

"I wanted to tell you . . ."

"And I've such a lot I want to tell you and I've got a present for you. Now change your shoes, I must see how you have got on."

Once Lydia had on her shoes she was never able to think of anything but her dancing. So as Miss Arrowhead called out instructions and Mrs. Bennett—as usual reading a paper at the same time—thumped away on the piano she worked hard and happily, conscious that she had honestly tried while Miss Arrowhead was away and that the repetition had done her good—or, at least, no harm.

At the end of the lesson Miss Arrowhead gave some of her rare praise.

"Excellent. My time away has been well spent. Now come here and look at this."

"This" was a native peasant dress which Miss Arrowhead had brought her. Lydia managed to make pleased noises but she felt her inside rushing round like a squirrel in a cage. At last she blurted out:

"Please, please, I've got something I must tell you."

Miss Arrowhead saw that Lydia was on the verge of tears. She dismissed Mrs. Bennett and pulled Lydia down beside her on to one of the studio benches.

"What's the trouble?"

Out the story poured. How, if Miss Arrowhead had not been away, she would not have been so desperate. How she had managed to see Monsieur de Clara. Of the awful punishment she had received. How she had taught Rosie her doll dance for ten and sixpence a lesson. How she had been invited to the audition. How she had planned to go by herself only her mother had found the box with the money. How she had intended to pretend she had toothache. How her mother had explained she never could learn with Monsieur de Clara because there was no money. How, even knowing there was no money, she simply had to go to the audition because if Monsieur de Clara chose her it would be something to remember always. How her mother had said she would take her to the audition but only if nobody except Miss Arrowhead knew, because Dad must never know because he would worry that he couldn't pay.

Miss Arrowhead listened to all this in silence. Then she said:

"I understand, Lydie, that you have to go on Monday. But I will take you. I shall telephone your mother to tell her this."

CHAPTER THIRTY

THE AUDITION

GEMMA was told that Lydia would not be at school on Monday—that Miss Arrowhead wanted her. Miss Arrowhead squared things with Mrs. Calvert. So on the Monday morning Lydia—her dancing things in a small case—and Miss Arrowhead caught the early train to London.

Because Lydia must not think planning to go to London alone was not a crime Alice had told Miss Arrowhead she wanted her to use her three pounds ten shillings for the expenses.

"Fortunately cheap day returns and Lydia is half price are not very expensive so, even allowing for taxis and something to eat, there should be enough. I don't want her to come back with any change."

Miss Arrowhead accepted this but Lydia was so tense and excited that she suggested she looked after the money as Lydia would be almost certain to lose it.

The Dickens Theatre was not far from the station so they had time for some coffee before the audition, not that Lydia wanted coffee, her one idea was to get to the theatre.

"We shall be late, I know we shall," she fussed as Miss Arrowhead sipped at her coffee and ate a biscuit.

"It isn't yet half-past ten," said Miss Arrowhead calmly. "It will be time enough if we are there at 10.45 and then I expect we'll have a long wait."

When they did reach the theatre the doorkeeper sent them to a dressing-room at the top of the building.

"You can't miss it," he told them, "there's a lot of

other young ladies changing up there. You'll be called when he wants you on the stage."

When they reached the dressing-room they found the room full of girls of varying ages accompanied either by their mothers or presumably their dancing teacher's. Miss Arrowhead looked round and found an unoccupied space with a piece of dressing-table on which to put Lydia's case and a hook for her clothes.

It did not take Lydia long to change into her pink tights and ballet shoes, her white tunic and pink belt. Then Miss Arrowhead helped with her hair, fastening it on top of her head held firmly in place with a pink ribbon.

"There seems," Miss Arrowhead whispered, "to be a variety of opinion about what should be worn at auditions."

Lydia looked round. There was indeed a variety. Most of the girls were much older than Lydia, almost if not quite, grown up she decided and these mostly wore leotards though some were wearing tunics, but the majority of those wearing tunics had thick woollen stockings pulled on over their tights to keep their legs warm. It was amongst the children that there was the variety of dress. Two wore tutus, one had a knee-length ballet frock, one had on what looked like a bathing dress and another a silk blouse and brief silk pleated skirt. The rest wore plain tunics like Lydia's.

"There are an awful lot of us being auditioned," Lydia whispered. "How many do you think Monsieur de Clara wants?"

They had made room for themselves to sit on a bench.

"I should think," said Miss Arrowhead, "there are two groups here. The older girls are probably hoping to join the ballet company."

"Then only us children want to be taught by him?"

"That's my guess," Miss Arrowhead agreed, "but we shall see."

Soon afterwards a woman came in with a list of names which she read out. It was a sort of roll call to see they were all there. Then she said:

"If you'll follow me, Monsieur de Clara will try you out in groups of three."

They trouped to the side of the stage. It was very cold so Lydia was glad Miss Arrowhead had made her carry her coat, but even with it on she was afraid of her muscles getting stiff. But Miss Arrowhead had thought of that.

"Come on. Limber up—nothing like a few pliés to keep you warm."

Monsieur de Clara, when he arrived, wasted no time. He called for the first three girls and gave them an enchaînement to dance. Out of the first three he had one back and made her dance again. Afterwards the woman who had called out their names talked to the girl, evidently taking down some details.

"I thought she had promise," said Miss Arrowhead. "The other two may as well give up."

Monsieur de Clara saw nine more girls before Lydia was called. Not, to her surprise, with two of the children but with two of the grown-ups. This did not worry Lydia —nothing worried her when she was dancing. She listened carefully to Monsieur de Clara's instructions, glad that they included pirouettes for she was good at pirouettes and in her turn she carried them out. When the third girl had finished the enchaînement Monsieur de Clara dismissed the other two but told Lydia to remain. He did not, as he had done previously, ask her to dance the enchaînement again but instead gave her a string of different steps. Lydia memorised them and danced them. When she had finished Monsieur de Clara beckoned to her.

"It was you I think who stole Minou."

"Not stole," said Lydia, "only borrowed and my goodness I was punished when I got home."

Monsieur de Clara nodded approvingly.

"Quite right. You were a bad girl and deserved punishment. Who teaches you to dance?"

Lydia pointed into the wings.

"Miss Arrowhead. She's there."

Monsieur de Clara gave a dismissing gesture.

"Run along, it is this Miss Arrowhead I wish to see."

Although Lydia was dying to know what Monsieur de Clara had said Miss Arrowhead refused to say a word until they were in a restaurant having lunch.

"Well?" Lydia asked.

"Well," replied Miss Arrowhead, "Monsieur de Clara was very complimentary to me as a teacher."

"But does he want to teach me?"

Miss Arrowhead was a long time answering.

"What he suggested was that I continued to teach you regularly but that you took two classes a week with him."

Lydia almost fell off her chair.

"He wants me! He wants me!"

"I did not," Miss Arrowhead went on. "explain it was impossible for you to attend his classes for that would have made him ask why you had wasted his time. But I said we would let him know."

That sobered Lydia.

"Don't let him know too soon, something might happen —miracles do."

Miss Arrowhead shook her head.

"Not this one, Lydie. He charges a lot for his lessons and there would be fares for you and whoever took you. You said all you wanted was to know if he would teach you. Well he would have. You must be contented with that."

"I know that's what I said." Lydia agreed. "But it's

not how I feel now. Learning with both you and him would be absolutely perfect. I won't be contented with that. I'll find a way to learn with him—you see if I don't."

CHAPTER THIRTY-ONE

ANN'S EYES OPEN

At half-term Ann was again on the Teenage Trend programme. Once more she stayed with the Stratfords and was taken to the performance by Mrs. Stratford. Barry Thomas met them there. This time Ann had a new frock bought with her own money to suit her own taste. It was silver grey, severely cut with a curiously quakerish look about it. Mrs. Stratford thought it was too plain but Audrey said it was smashing and Barry Thomas was enraptured with it.

"You'll be setting a fashion," he said, "unless you're careful. I can see frocks advertised as the 'Ann Robinson line'."

For Ann, except that she did not like "If you were me" as much as she had liked "Rose-coloured World", the performance was very like the last. Had she known enough about what was going on she would have noticed that she had special treatment for she was now a recognised star. But to Ann it was just an evening to be got through made bearable because, if the song was popular, she could buy such a lot more musical instruments for the mentally handicapped.

"You put that over well and the kids ate it," said Barry Thomas when she had finished singing.

"Do you think it will make the charts?" Ann asked.

Barry was amused.

"Are you becoming a careerist suddenly?"

"Not really," Ann confessed, "but I know if it's in the charts I make more money. Most of what I earn Dad puts in a bank for me but most of what's over I use for a school thing."

"I'm not a prophet," Barry said, "but I'd guess you'd hit it, though I doubt that song reaching the top."

This time when Ann and Mrs. Stratford reached home Audrey had watched the programme. She was full of enthusiasm.

"You were gorgeous, Ann, and your dress looked really good. I can't think what you want to go to a university for when you can sing like that."

Ann laughed.

"And I can't see why you want to be a ski instructor."

"Well, what I say is," said Mrs. Stratford, "it's lucky you don't all want the same things or there wouldn't be the jobs to go round."

While Ann was in London Gemma was having her first fitting for her dress for Juliet. It was an over-dress and an under-dress and there was a cloak and various veils, wreaths and other attachments to show change of scene. The whole dress was white, the outer dress of a brocade woven with silver flowers, the inner was made of chiffon. The dress, like all the others worn in the play, had been designed in an art school, but they were being made in the university.

Although the Dulcie row had died down Gemma was always conscious of being an outsider in the university except when she was on the stage. She had gone to this first fitting with trepidation but she need not have bothered, the group who were making the clothes were enthusiasts at their job.

"Well," said one speaking through a mouth full of pins, "this isn't going to look too bad."

"It's very young looking," agreed another girl who was crawling round Gemma measuring the hem.

"What colour is Romeo wearing?" Gemma asked.

"Blue," said the girl with the pins. "Sort of midnight blue. You ought to look fine together."

"Funny," remarked the girl on the floor, "only a short time back the performance seemed aeons away—now here we are in March and in two months it'll all be over."

Gemma shivered. Two months and it would all be over. No John Cann. No Headstone. No family. Just her and Mummy. Oh dear, why couldn't she live in two places at once?

"Are we keeping you standing too long?" asked the girl with the pins. "You're trembling."

"No, I'm O.K. . . . thank you," said Gemma. "I think, as my cousins' grandmother would say, a goose walked over my grave."

Ann came back from her week-end with Audrey on the Monday evening. She had enjoyed herself very much and was bursting to tell the family all she had done. She was not expecting to be met because Philip was giving a lesson so she caught a bus which dropped her near Trelawny Drive.

There was a note for her from her mother on the hall table.

"Hope you had a wonderful time. We thought you were grand. Lydie is at a party. Robin I need hardly tell you is spending the day with Nigs. Gemma—as you know—is having a fitting. I'll be back as soon as I can. Love. Mum."

Ann went into the kitchen to put on the kettle to make herself some tea then, while it boiled, she took her case upstairs to unpack it. Outside her bedroom door she stood still to listen. Surely somewhere she heard a sound— either a cough or a choke. She put down her case and opened Robin's door. The room was in its usual state of confusion but no Robin. Then she went to the foot of the ladder leading up to Lydia's room. She was going to call out to ask if she was there but there was no need, Lydia was there but she was not coughing or choking, she was crying.

Quickly Ann ran up the ladder and looked into the room. Lydia was lying face downwards on the bed sobbing as if her heart would break. Ann sat down on the bed beside her.

"What's up Lydie?"

"What's up, Lydie?"

Lydia rolled over displaying a face crimson and blotched with crying. In a very nosey way she gasped out:

"I wasn't expectin' you for simbly ages."

Ann gave Lydia her handkerchief.

"Mum said you were at a party."

"I was meant to be," Lydia sniffed, "but I was too miserable to go."

"Miserable about what?" Ann asked.

Lydia blew her nose.

"That's what's so awful. I can't tell you or anybody. Mum made me promise I wouldn't before I went."

Ann couldn't make head or tail of that.

"Went where?"

"Just somewhere—I can't tell you any more. But inside I'm as miserable as miserable and I never can cry because someone's always there. But today I was alone getting ready for the party and I started to cry and couldn't stop."

Ann's mind was turning over possibilities. What had Lydie to cry about? Only one thing would make her cry. It must be to do with her dancing.

"I've put on a kettle," she said. "Come down to the kitchen and have some tea. It will make you feel better."

Lydia got off the bed.

"Nothing could make me feel that, but I would like some tea."

Ann made the tea and cut some bread and butter. She talked about Teenage Trend and what it was like staying with the Stratfords but her mind was on Lydia. She must find out what was wrong. Presently, when Lydia was better she said:

"I suppose it is to do with your dancing."

"Why do you think that?" Lydia demanded. "I didn't say so."

"Don't be an ass," said Ann. "What else makes you cry? Is it to do with Miss Arrowhead? Is she going away again?"

"No. I can't tell you, Ann. You see I promised Mum I wouldn't."

Suddenly Ann saw daylight.

"Is it to do with that Monsieur de Clara you ran away to see that day we went to London?"

Lydia looked at Ann over her cup.

"I didn't tell you that."

"Of course not," Ann agreed, "but now I've guessed you might as well tell me the rest. I won't pass it on, you know that."

As if floodgates had opened out poured the story. Of teaching Rosie to dance to earn the money. Of how the audition notice came and she had meant to sneak off alone only Mum had found the money. Of the audition and what Monsieur de Clara had said. Of how she had said she only wanted to know if Monsieur de Clara would teach her—but when she knew he would how Miss Arrowhead had said she must be contented with knowing. But how she couldn't be—then crying again she gulped:

"And now Miss Arrowhead says I've got to write this week to say I can't learn with him. I can't bear it. I can't bear it. He's the greatest teacher in the whole world."

Ann sat staring at Lydia's heaving shoulders. Then she said:

"But why didn't you ask me? You know my record makes money."

Lydia raised her streaming face.

"Why should I ask you? You give all your money to the school charity."

"But you might at least have asked me. I can't guess what you want."

"But if you know you don't do anything. Look how much Robin wants and wants a honky-tonk piano. You knew that."

Ann felt as if she had been living in a chrysalis and it was splitting open. "If you know you don't do anything." It was true. And all this time she had thought she was doing so well. Helping with money at home. Providing a mass of instruments for the mentally handicapped—and yet she had never thought to ask what a honky-tonk piano cost. She got up.

156

"I must unpack. But don't fuss. You can have your two lessons a week from Monsieur de Clara. I'll pay."

CHAPTER THIRTY-TWO

ROMEO AND JULIET

IT was a Sunday in May. A particularly lovely May with young green on all the trees, tulips in every garden and lilac bursting into flower. Even Gemma managed to drag herself away from Juliet long enough to notice all the beauty.

"Oh dear! Headstone is looking so nice. I shall miss being here when I'm in London."

"Nonsense!" said Philip. "Nothing is more beautiful than a London park in the spring."

Gemma smiled at him.

"All right, I know. It's going to be grand living with Mummy but you can't talk me out of missing you all because I shall."

"Not me you won't," said Lydia, "if I'm coming to lunch with you on dancing class days."

"Nor me," Ann pointed out, "if I'm going to stay with you every time I make a record."

"So really," Robin said, "it's mostly me you won't see, but I bet you soon will. My swirling sounds super on my honky-tonk—I'm sure I'll soon be as famous as Ann."

Alice gave Gemma a loving look.

"And you're not getting rid of me, for it looks as if it will usually be me who takes Lydie up to her classes."

Philip nodded.

"That's right though if I can get away I might sneak up to London occasionally."

They were having supper. Gemma looked round the table at them all.

"Do you remember that first day I came here? I never, never thought then I'd be part of the family."

"Nor did we," said Robin. "You were a very toffee-nosed type."

Philip laughed.

"That's enough of raking up Gemma's past."

"Anyway if you've finished eating, Gemma," said Alice, "I'm afraid it's bed for you. Tomorrow will be a heavy day."

"Romeo and Juliet" was being performed for a week. There had already been three dress rehearsals, the last on the Saturday. But Monday was the great first night with, it was rumoured, critics present from all the national papers. The mere thought of them made Gemma's knees knock together for she knew she had still such a lot to learn as a Shakespearean actress.

Mrs. Calvert had decided that Gemma should spend the day in school as usual.

"She'll be better here with us," Mrs. Calvert had told Alice on the telephone. "She'll only get more nervous alone at home and I can see she has a rest in the afternoon."

School was not much help. Each time she thought of the evening ahead of her Gemma's inside felt as if it was going down in a lift. She implored not to be made to rest.

"I shall only feel worse," she told Mrs. Calvert. "I keep thinking 'suppose I forget my lines'."

"Why on earth should you?" Mrs. Calvert asked cheerfully. "You've been working at them long enough and you are a good study. But if you should there is always the prompter."

"Suppose there's another row about Dulcie?"

"There won't be," said Mrs. Calvert. "Young Dulcie

158

looks magnificent as Lady Capulet and knows it. I don't think she would play Juliet now if she was offered the part."

Mrs. Calvert put Gemma to rest on her bed. Now she pulled down the blinds.

"Try and think of something else," she advised. "Try and remember the lines you spoke when you acted Lady Jane Grey."

Curiously enough this treatment worked. It was quite hard to remember Lady Jane, Gemma had acted the part so long ago. Presently she was repeating "Yes, my lady mother" over and over again. Then she was asleep.

At last it was time to go to the theatre. Mrs. Calvert was acting as Gemma's dresser and with them in the car came the girl who was understudying Gemma. She was a nice sensible girl and, knowing Gemma was nervous, she talked calmly to Mrs. Calvert about school things just as if it were an ordinary day.

Never afterwards could Gemma remember clearly that first night. She could remember standing in the wings wearing her under-frock with a kind of surcoat over it held in place by a jewelled girdle. She could remember hearing the scene start with Dulcie as Lady Capulet saying:

"Nurse, where's my daughter? call her forth to me."

Then the nurse answered and she was on stage. The rest was a blank until, her heart beating suffocatingly, she first met Romeo in the great chamber. Then it was as she had known it would be—just her and Romeo until the end. She forgot the audience entirely until she, with Romeo holding her hand, with the rest of the cast was bowing to them.

Though Gemma did not know it at the time, she and John Cann made theatrical history that night. Headstone University was talked about wherever theatre was discussed. And Gemma's fourteen-year-old Juliet went into the pages of theatrical history. Already, before the first cheers had died away, it was known the week in Headstone was not to be the end of the production. London was to see it and probably Stratford-on-Avon.

*　　*　　*

All the family came to see Gemma off at the station. She departed as she had arrived—surrounded by luggage which the porter put in a first-class carriage.

"You've certainly made your mark in Headstone," Philip said as he kissed her. "We're proud of you."

Ann hugged Gemma.

"I shall miss you awfully. Truly I shall."

Lydia was turning a pirouette.

"Don't get too grand when we aren't there to keep you in your place."

Robin opened the carriage door for her.

"You better get in, the guard's got his flag out."

"Darling," said Alice reaching up to kiss Gemma. "So it's really good-bye and I hate it."

Robin conducted Ann and Lydia:

"O dear, what can the matter be?
O dear, what can the matter be?
O dear, what can the matter be?
Gemma has gone to the town."

Then the train began to move and the family waved: "Good-bye, Gemma. Good-bye. Good-bye. Good-bye."